Sandwell
Metropolitan Borough Council

Please return this item to any Sandwell Library on or before
the return date.

You may renew the item unless it has been reserved by
another borrower.

You can renew your library items by using the 24/7 renewal
hotline number - 0845 352 4949
or FREE online at opac-lib.sandwell.gov.uk

THANK YOU FOR USING YOUR LIBRARY

D0550947

HER MISTLETOE
COWBOY

BY
MARIE FERRARELLA

All rights reserved including the right of reproduction in whole or in part in any form. This edition is published by arrangement with Harlequin Enterprises II B.V./S.à.r.l. The text of this publication or any part thereof may not be reproduced or transmitted in any form or by any means, electronic or mechanical, including photocopying, recording, storage in an information retrieval system, or otherwise, without the written permission of the publisher.

This book is sold subject to the condition that it shall not, by way of trade or otherwise, be lent, resold, hired out or otherwise circulated without the prior consent of the publisher in any form of binding or cover other than that in which it is published and without a similar condition including this condition being imposed on the subsequent purchaser.

® and ™ are trademarks owned and used by the trademark owner and/or its licensee. Trademarks marked with ® are registered with the United Kingdom Patent Office and/or the Office for Harmonisation in the Internal Market and in other countries.

First published in Great Britain 2013
By Mills & Boon, an imprint of Harlequin (UK) Limited,
Eton House, 18-24 Paradise Road, Richmond, Surrey, TW9 1SR

© Marie Rydzynski-Ferrarella 2012

ISBN: 978 0 263 25188 3

Published in Great Britain 2015
by Mills & Boon, an imprint of Harlequin (UK) Limited,
Eton House, 18-24 Paradise Road, Richmond, Surrey, TW9 1SR

© 2015 Marie Rydzynski-Ferrarella

ISBN: 978-0-263-25188-3

23-1215

Harlequin (UK) Limited's policy is to use papers that are natural, renewable and recyclable products and made from wood grown in sustainable forests. The logging and manufacturing processes conform to the legal environmental regulations of the country of origin.

Printed and bound in Spain
by CPI, Barcelona

Marie Ferrarella, a *USA TODAY* bestselling and RITA®
Award–winning author has written more than two hundred and fifty books for Mills & Boon, some under the
name Marie Nicole. Her romances are beloved by fans
worldwide. Visit her website, www.marieferrarella.com.

To Father Anthony
of
St. Joseph's Indian School

Thank you for all you've done
and
keep up the good work!

Prologue

"No."

Stunned, Garrett White Eagle stared at his older brother, Jackson. He'd just checked his email and when he read the notification from the editor in chief of a well-known magazine, asking to do an in-depth article on the work he and his brother were doing at the Healing Ranch, he thought that Jackson would be as excited about it as he was.

Obviously not.

This was going to take some work on his part, Garrett decided.

"No?" he repeated incredulously. "What do you mean, no?"

Jackson rose from behind the scarred, second-hand desk he'd rescued from being turned into kindling half a dozen years ago. He had a full day ahead of him at the ranch and he'd already wasted enough time with the stack of unpaid bills that seemed to be breeding on his desk. Apparently, moving them from one pile to another didn't diminish their number or get them paid off any sooner.

He couldn't think about them right now. The boys were waiting for him at the corral. The bunkhouse was almost filled to capacity and every teen currently staying at the ranch required individual care. He'd sworn when he took all this on that nothing short of that would suffice and he had meant it. But it did get hard to live up to at times.

"No," Jackson repeated. "It's a simple enough word to grasp." The corners of his mouth curved just the slightest bit as he glanced toward his younger brother. "Even you, with your limited education, should be able to figure out its meaning."

"Look, I get it. You're not into social media. But I'm not asking you to get on Twitter, or Facebook, or any of the other modern innovations you keep insisting on staying clear of. I'm not even asking you to use smoke signals, like our ancestors. But to turn your back on a magazine interview is positively criminal," Garrett accused. "*Western Times* is a *big-time magazine*," he emphasized, as if the increased volume would somehow get his brother to agree. This was an opportunity and he wasn't about to give up until he made Jackson see the light. He had his work cut out for him, seeing as Jackson could bring new meaning to the word *stubborn* when he wanted to.

Jackson turned around for a split second, looking his brother in the eye and enunciating every word slowly. "I can't make time for it."

"Do you have time to make money?" Garrett asked. "How about that? Do you have time to do that?"

Jackson stifled an impatient sigh. "What are you talking about? They're not paying us for the interview."

"No, but doing the interview could really pay off in the long run." Garrett picked up his pace to keep up with Jackson.

Just like when we were younger, he couldn't help remembering. Back then, he'd worshipped Jackson, who was five years his senior. Technically, Jackson was his half brother. They shared a father who wasn't interested in either of them. Ben White Eagle walked out on them just the way Jackson's mother had walked out on him several years before that. It was his own mother who was left with the task of raising both of them.

Sylvia White Eagle was a warm, loving woman who more than had her hands filled with a very hostile, rebellious Jackson. Jackson was always rushing off to be with his friends, friends who were interested in grabbing what life hadn't given them. Friends who kept getting him into more and more trouble.

Desperate, Sylvia had turned to Sam, her ex-husband's brother, and Sam had taken Jackson in hand, putting him to work on his ranch. It was there that Jackson got his life back.

As for Garrett, he had joined Jackson and his uncle when his mother died. They worked the ranch together and when Sam passed away, he had left the ranch to both of them.

It was Jackson's idea to start up the Healing Ranch, creating it in Sam's honor. There Jackson and Garrett put Sam's methods to work, using horses as a way to get through to misguided, wayward boys and make them come around rather than turning into hardened criminals.

Since its slow start, the ranch had been growing increasingly successful. Despite that, it wasn't making any money, but that was because Jackson, ever mindful of the dire circumstances some people found themselves in, only charged what he felt the parents or guardians who came to him as their last hope could afford to pay. But their bills to run the ranch just kept on growing.

From what Jackson had let slip recently, they couldn't be ignored too much longer.

And now, Garrett thought, it seemed that Fortune had decided to smile on the Healing Ranch—except that Jackson refused to see it that way.

Garrett was determined not to have him pass up on what just might be their one chance to make things work.

He blew out a frustrated breath. Jackson apparently had stopped paying any attention to the conversation he thought he was having with his brother.

"The Saunders kid is finally ready to get in the saddle," Jackson was saying as he walked toward the front door.

Garrett hurried after him. Spotting Debi in the living room, Garrett immediately enlisted his sister-in-law as an ally. "Debi, talk some sense into this lunkhead you married," he pleaded.

The blonde, green-eyed nurse willingly obliged. "Lunkhead, listen to your brother." Debi smiled at Garrett as she lifted her shoulders in a helpless shrug. "I tried. By the way, what's he supposed to be listening to?"

"The voice of reason," Garrett answered, doing his best to keep his temper.

"Ha!" was Jackson's response. He looked at his wife of three months, appealing for her to back him up. "He wants some woman to come out and follow us around, asking a bunch of questions, snooping and getting in the way."

"Auditioning for a wife, Garrett?" Debi asked her brother-in-law, amused.

"No point. Jackson's already snatched away the love of my life," Garrett replied with a good-natured wink. And then he grew serious. "I'm just trying to find a way to keep the wolf from the door."

As down to earth as her husband, Debi took an active interest in the monetary issues that went into running the school. It was the school that had initially brought her here, looking for a way to get through to her younger brother before he destroyed himself. If possible, she was even more dedicated to keeping the ranch operating than either of the brothers.

"Keep talking," she urged Garrett.

Jackson groaned. "Don't encourage him."

But Garrett was quick to get his sister-in-law to join forces with him. He felt confident that Jackson wouldn't say no to her. "*Western Times Magazine* wants to send a writer to come out and do a story about the ranch."

Surprised, Debi turned toward her husband. "That's wonderful!"

"What's wonderful about it?" Jackson asked. "I've got a ranch to run, I don't have time to answer a bunch of questions."

"Then don't," Debi told him simply. Before Jackson could say something about being vindicated or Garrett could complain that he thought that she would have been on his side, she came through with the natural solution. "Have Garrett do it. He's a lot more outgoing than you are, anyway."

Jackson pretended to scowl. "Thanks."

Debi hooked her arm through his, looking up into

his eyes. Her own were sparkling with humor. "But you have all these other fine qualities."

"I guess I do at that." Jackson laughed, allowing himself one quick kiss before he looked at his brother. "Okay, call them and tell 'em she can come."

This time it was Garrett's turn to kiss Debi, planting one on her cheek. "Bless the day you came here, Debi! I'll call them right now before Smiley here changes his mind!"

And with that Garrett raced up the stairs to his room and his computer.

Chapter One

"Really? You're serious? Two weeks before Christmas and you're sending me to Siberia?" Kimberly Lee cried, appalled and stunned.

"Forever, Texas," Stan Saunders corrected her tranquilly.

The editor in chief of *Western Times Magazine*, as well as several other magazines that came under the Union-Post Publishing masthead, was known for his calm, almost monotone demeanor. He had a voice to match. It never rose above a certain level, no matter what was being said or how upset the person on the receiving end might be.

As was the case with Kim, who had asked to see the editor in chief in order to score an assignment for one of the magazines he oversaw. At the time she definitely hadn't set her sights on an article for *Western Times Magazine*, in her opinion the least sophisticated of the magazines in the array.

She'd grown more and more stunned as Stan described the article he wanted and the place that he was sending her to.

"Same thing," Kim complained. Grasping the armrests, she moved to the edge of the chair she'd taken in his glass-enclosed office. "Look, I know I'm just a lowly freelance writer—"

"Yes, you are," Stan agreed all too readily, indicating that she had made her point for him.

Refusing to be deterred, Kim forged on. "But you've *got* to have some other story than this you want me to write."

She stopped just short of pleading, aware that Stan had no use for that sort of tactic. She'd been writing for Stan for a little over a year now, coming in twice a month to see what sort of articles were up for grabs. Each magazine had its own small in-house stable of writers. The slack was taken up by freelance writers who were eager, like her, to prove their worth while earning extra pocket money. Most stitched together a living—if that was their goal rather than just some additional income—by making the rounds to various publishers, as well as haunting blog-oriented websites.

"No, I don't," Stan told her. "It's either this, or come back in a couple of weeks."

She sighed. "I don't have a couple of weeks. My rent check is due now—not to mention that in a couple of weeks, it'll be Christmas and last year, there was nothing to be had," she reminded him.

There was just a hint of concern on the crusty, bald man's face as he asked, "Can't hit up Mom and Dad for the money?"

Kim knew he was aware of her backstory. At least, as much as she'd told to him. Whether or not he remembered it, given how many writers he dealt with, was another matter.

Giving him the benefit of the doubt, she pretended he remembered. "And have them look at me with pity in their eyes?" She shook her head emphatically. "I'd rather die first."

Stan inclined his head, conceding the point. "Fair enough. How about those two successful sisters of yours? Didn't you tell me they were surgeons or something like that? They must have money they can lend their little sister."

Monica and Maureen would have more than readily given her the money she needed, but they were like her parents, convinced that she should have done something better with her life and if nothing else, should now be running, not walking, to the nearest university to enroll and get herself on track for a *real* career, not one that was grounded in make-believe.

That was how her whole family viewed her career path—chasing after make-believe.

More than anything, ever since she could remember, she had dreamed of being a writer, an *important* writer who would someday write that one book people would always remember. Not for a week, or a month, but one that would live on through the decades, a book that would make a real *difference* to people.

In the meantime, she had resigned herself to the fact that she had bills to pay, so any work she could get as a freelance writer had to make do for now.

Almost any work, she silently amended. There *had* to be something else, some other article that didn't involve sagebrush and horses and brawny, uneducated cowboys.

"See the above answer," Kim quipped regarding asking her sisters for help.

Stan believed in being helpful, but only up to a point. That point did not include fabricating work for his writers, even if he had come to secretly like their spirit, and

Kim was nothing if not the embodiment of that old-fashioned term, *spunk*.

"Well, unless you have a rich sugar daddy tucked away somewhere, or are planning on selling your soul to the devil by midnight to keep that old wolf from the door, I'd say you'd better get busy, pack up your go-bag and book a flight to Laredo."

"Laredo?" she repeated, confused. "I thought you said that I was going to some place in Texas called Farewell."

"Forever," Stan corrected patiently. "And your hearing's good. You are."

She didn't get it. "If I'm going to Forever, why am I flying to Laredo?"

"Simple," he told her. "Forever doesn't have an airport. You're going to have to rent a car and drive the rest of the way. Keep your receipts," he advised. "There's a little extra in petty cash. I'll see what I can do about reimbursing you for some of that."

This was beginning to sound better and better, she thought, exasperated.

"Do they have indoor plumbing?" she asked. She was only half kidding.

Stan never cracked a smile. "So I hear." He raised his deep-set eyes to hers. "I also hear they've built a hotel."

Why was he telling her that? "Is there something unusual about it?"

Thin, bony shoulders rose and fell beneath a light gray shirt that appeared to have been slept in at least a couple of times. "Not that I know."

Okay, she still wasn't enlightened about the point of this conversation.

"Then why are you...?" And then it hit her. "Wait,

you don't mean that they didn't have hotels there before this one."

This time, he did allow a small smile to edge out. "That's exactly what I mean."

"What kind of a hellhole *is* this place?" she cried.

"The kind of hellhole where kids whose parents think there's no reaching them get turned around and become the decent people they were always meant to be." The editor paused for a long moment, as if silently debating something with himself. Finally, in the same low-key voice he always used, he said, "My nephew, Jordy, is there."

Kim's dark brown eyes widened. He'd told her it was a sort of reformatory school with horses. That meant his nephew was one of those troubled delinquents he'd mentioned.

"I'm so sorry." She assumed that would be the response Stan was expecting.

But the editor surprised her by saying, "Don't be. That place is the best thing that could have happened to him." The most genuine smile she'd ever seen was curving Stan's lips as he went on to tell her, "My sister Paula said Jordy actually called home last week. Told me he sounded more like himself than he had in the last three years. She was crying those ridiculous happy tears at the time, the ones that you women use to confuse men.

"A place that can do that for a kid, for a family," he went on to say, "well, other people deserve to know about it." He grew very serious now as he looked at her. "You want to do an important story? *This* is an important story," he told her with emphasis. "Go do it and do it right." It was more of an order than an instruction. "You do a good enough job, then we'll talk about where your career could go with the magazines I edit when you get back."

She warned herself not to get excited. There was always a downside to everything. She just hadn't heard all of it yet. "Is that anything like dangling a carrot in front of me?"

"Carrot?" Stan echoed. He permitted himself a dismissive snort. "More like the whole damn bushel. Open your eyes, Lee, and take in the whole picture. I'm giving you a chance here."

Kim tightened her hands on the armrests and pushed herself up to her feet. She knew Stan. She wasn't going to get a better offer no matter how much she battered him. It was up to her to turn what really sounded like a fluff piece to her into something golden. "Then I guess I'm off," she told him.

The phone on his desk was ringing. Stan covered the receiver with his wide, spidery hand, waiting to pick it up.

"Yes, you are," he acknowledged just before he picked up the receiver.

This wasn't just another state, Kim thought as she drove the compact tan Toyota she'd rented at the airport, it was another world. Some parallel universe that perversely coexisted beside the modern, sophisticated one to which she had not only been born, but where she thrived and definitely preferred being.

San Francisco had been home to her for all of her twenty-eight years, and while some of the people she knew claimed to actively love "getting away from it all" by doing things like going camping and hiking in the mountains, the thought of being somewhere where sidewalks were only a theory, not a genuine fact of life, seemed somehow barbaric to her.

Even in her teens, she had never had a desire to be "one with the earth" or to even mildly pretend to be "roughing it." To her, roughing it meant doing without her cell phone or her laptop for half a day and even that made her feel more than vaguely uncomfortable, as if she had lost her hold on civilization, her connection to the outside world.

Which was what she was beginning to feel as she traveled down what she supposed amounted to a two-lane road to this town that seemed to mean so much to Saunders. A town that some of the maps didn't even have listed.

Kim could feel a sense of desperation beginning to build up within her.

"Brigadoon, Stan is sending me to Brigadoon," she muttered under her breath, thinking of the village in the musical revival her mother had all but dragged her to when she was only about nine.

Looking back, she recalled that her mother was always trying to infuse a love of music and culture into her three daughters. Monica and Maureen had lapped it up. She remembered feeling that a play about a town that popped up every hundred years for a day's time before disappearing again was dumb, not to mention scary. Her mother had called her hopeless; her father had come to her defense, calling her a free thinker. But eventually, even he had given up on her.

Both her parents, she knew, wanted her to "be somebody." Her sisters had both followed their example, or at least their father's example. David Lee was a well-respected neurosurgeon at the prestigious UCSF Medical Center and each of her sisters had their own surgical specialties and enjoyed surgery privileges at the same hospital, making her father exceedingly proud.

Her mother was a law professor at the University of San Francisco. Her classes were always in demand. Which made her, with her BA in Liberal Arts—emphasis on English—the official black sheep of the family.

"You'd think, with an Asian-American father and a mother whose grandparents hailed from Ireland and Scotland, and came here eager to make something of themselves in their adopted county, you'd have some real drive, some kind of ambition to become someone," her mother had lamented when she had informed her parents that she was not applying to either medical school or law school.

Well, she had drive. Only her drive just happened to be in another direction than her parents and sisters had taken.

A drive that was stalling, Kim thought in disgust, with this detour to write a story about a town that was barely a visible dot on the map.

She would have been tempted to say that Stan had made the whole thing up, playing some really bizarre belated April Fool's prank on her two weeks before Christmas—except that she had actually managed to find the damn hole-in-the-wall on her GPS when she'd gotten into the car she'd rented at the airport.

The airport at Laredo had been all right, she supposed. Nothing like what she was used to in San Francisco, but compared to what she was looking at now on her way to Forever, the airport seemed like an absolute Shangri-la.

How did people *survive* in places like this? And why

would they even *want* to if they had to live out their whole lives here? Kim couldn't help wondering. There were miles and miles of miles and miles, nothing else in either direction.

All she knew was that if she'd been born in a place like this, she would have saved every dime she could and the moment she graduated high school, she would have been gone—maybe even before then if the opportunity presented itself—but definitely the second she graduated.

There was nothing out here except for desolation, with an occasional ranch thrown in between, but she hadn't even seen one of *those* for an hour now.

People who lived in this part of the country probably looked like dried-up, wrinkled prunes by the time they were thirty-five, she estimated, glancing up toward the sky through her windshield.

Not wanting to usher in the dust, she had her windows rolled up and soon discovered that it was warm in her car. The weather down here was a lot warmer than she was accustomed to this time of year. She shouldn't have wasted her time packing heavy sweaters and jackets, she thought.

You shouldn't have wasted your time coming here at all, a nagging voice in her head that sounded suspiciously like her sister, Monica, whispered to her. *Mom and Dad would have been more than happy to lend you the money—or better yet, have you move back into the house. It's way too big for just the two of them.*

Great, now she was hearing voices. More specifically, Monica's voice.

That was all she needed, to get heatstroke out here,

Kim thought in exasperation. Next, she would start hallucinating.

Damn it, she should have held out. There had to be some other story on Stan's docket, something she could have worked on that was a lot closer to home than this. Union-Post Publishing owned a theater magazine, didn't it? Stan could have easily sent her to do some puff piece on the new theater season that was coming next fall. Anything other than this Sagebrush Cowboys Save Troubled Teens thing he wanted her to write.

With every passing minute, she grew more irritable.

She should have stood her ground and dug in. Now it was too late and she was stuck out here. Stuck going to some stupid town called Farewell, or Forever, or Four Miles From Nowhere—

Kim's eyes widened as she stared at the small rectangular screen on the dashboard that had, until a moment ago, been her GPS monitoring unit.

Except now it wasn't.

It wasn't anything.

The screen had gone blank. Desperate, Kim hit the blank screen with the heel of her hand, trying to make it come around. It remained blank.

That was what she got for renting a compact car, she upbraided herself.

Trying to figure out what to do, she pulled the car over to the side of the road—although if she just kept on going, what was the difference? she asked herself. It wasn't as if she'd hit anything. There was nothing for her to hit in either direction, not even a rabbit, or snail, or whatever animals they had out here in the forgotten desert.

With the car idling, Kim shifted in her seat and pulled

her purse back onto the passenger seat. Her purse had lunged onto the floor when she'd pulled over a bit too suddenly, spilling, she now saw, its entire contents onto the floor of the car. Everything was in a jumbled heap.

Swallowing a curse, she pulled it all together and deposited it back into her purse—all except for her cell phone. That she took and opened. She swiped past a couple of screens until she found the GPS app that had come preinstalled on her phone.

Despite the fact that she'd lived her entire life in San Francisco, she still managed to get lost on a fairly regular basis and she had come to rely rather heavily on her phone's GPS feature.

A feature which wasn't pulling up, Kim noticed angrily as she stabbed over and over again at the small square image on her phone. When the image finally did enlarge, the words below it irritatingly informed her that it couldn't find a data connection and thus, the very sophisticated feature on her phone containing all the latest bells and whistles wasn't about to ring any of its bells or blow any of its whistles, at least not now. Not until its lost signal was suddenly restored.

"Damn it, I really am in hell," Kim declared, looking around.

There were absolutely no signs posted anywhere to tell her if she was going in the right direction or even if she was going around in circles. For all she knew, she wasn't even in Texas anymore.

The dirt road was too dry and hard to have registered her tire tracks, so she had no idea if she *had* traveled this way before.

"I could be going around in circles until I die from dehydration out here, and nobody'd know the difference—not even me," she lamented.

Why had she ever said yes to this horrible assignment?

For two cents, she'd turn around and go back—except that she had no idea if turning around actually *meant* that she was going back. Maybe if she turned around, she would eventually wind up driving into this town she didn't want to go to?

Damn it, she was confusing herself.

Feeling panicky, Kim looked around the interior of the pristine vehicle to see if there was anything packed in one of the side pockets that could help her.

After foraging around, she discovered an old folded map tucked into the side of the rear passenger door, but when she opened it, she found that the map did her no good. A product of the digital age, she had absolutely no idea how to actually *read* a map.

She was going to die out here, Kim thought, tossing the map aside. She was going to die out here and most likely, no one would ever even find her body.

She still stubbornly didn't regret not going to her parents for money. If she had to die, she would die rebellious and proud.

What did it feel like, she wondered, baking to death inside a low-end economy car? Maybe she should have rented something more high-end, like a Mercedes or a Jaguar. If it was going to wind up being her casket, then maybe—

A flash of something on the hill in the distance caught her eye.

Kim sat up, trying to focus as a glimmer of hope surfaced.

Was that a hallucination, or—?

Chapter Two

Damn but it was hot. This had to be the hottest December day to hit the area as far back as he could remember.

Taking off his tan Stetson, Garrett wiped his brow with the back of his hand, then put his hat back on. For what it was worth, the hat helped keep the sun out of his eyes.

He'd come up on this hill because it afforded him a better view of the surrounding terrain. The road below was flatter than his uncle's voice had been when Sam had sung in the occasional choir, back in the day. To his and Jackson's surprise, the man had been a big believer in going to church and he had made sure to usher the two of them in with him every Sunday.

Even now, he wasn't sure if Sam had exactly been a man of faith, or just someone who believed in the healing power of having a place to go where you were forced to think outside of yourself. Church had perhaps been that place for Sam.

Maybe that wouldn't have been good for some, but it certainly turned out to be good for Jackson and for him, Garrett thought now, still carefully scanning the road below. He would have hated to think where he and his brother would have wound up if it hadn't been for Sam and his rather strict way of doing things.

One thing was for sure, if it hadn't been for Sam, he wouldn't be here right now, looking for a long-overdue magazine writer.

According to the phone call he'd taken from the main editor of the bimonthly magazine doing that story on the Healing Ranch, the writer he'd sent, a woman named Kimberly Lee, should have gotten to them by now. The man who'd called an hour ago said he'd tried to reach her cell phone and received the message that it was out of range—something that was all too familiar around here. The editor had decided to call the ranch.

"She might have gotten lost," the man, a Stan Saunders, had told him. "I told her to get a car with a GPS, but even if she did, it's still possible that she's gotten lost. I called the airport rental agency and they said she rented a tan compact Toyota," he'd added as an afterthought.

The editor had started to recite the license plate to him, but he'd stopped the man, saying it was enough that he had a description of the car. There weren't exactly an abundance of compact Toyotas of any color in this part of Texas.

"People tend to drive Jeeps and trucks out here," he'd told the man. "But to be on the safe side, maybe you could describe your writer to me."

Saunders had immediately rattled off the pertinent details as if he was staring at a picture of the writer. "Kim's five-two, twenty-eight years old, has really dark brown eyes, blue-black hair, straight, chin length, oh, and she's Eurasian, if that helps any," he said as if he'd just remembered the last detail.

"I'll find her," he'd promised the man, more than a little intrigued now by the mental picture he'd formed from Saunders's description.

Before he left, he'd stopped to tell Jackson where he was going because this was the morning he was supposed to be overseeing some of the recent arrivals' progress. Now, because of the missing writer, Jackson was going to have to double up and take his boys, as well as his own.

Not that his brother minded extra work when it came to the teens on the ranch. That was, after all, the entire point of the ranch's existence. But he could see that Jackson minded the *reason* for his being unavailable for a while.

Ordinarily easygoing and unflappable, Jackson had frowned at the prospect of his going out to hunt for the supposedly missing writer.

"If you hadn't said yes to the story in the first place," Jackson had pointed out, "you wouldn't have to go running around, trying to track down the whereabouts of some displaced big-city tenderfoot who could just have gotten herself really lost out there."

"It'll all be worth it in the end," he'd promised Jackson just before he'd gone off.

Of course, he hadn't been all that sure about it at the moment.

And he still wasn't any surer about finding her now. Granted that looking for a tan compact foreign car was somewhat better than looking for a needle in the haystack—but not by much. There was a lot of terrain to cover between Forever and Laredo, and if this woman was really as bad at following directions as that editor had said she was, he just might have to enlist Sheriff Santiago and his deputies to help him find her.

What kind of a Navajo brave are you?

He could almost hear his uncle growling the question at him in that hoarse, gravelly voice of his.

Unlike a great many residents in and around the reservation that was located ten miles outside of Forever, Sam White Eagle had been very proud of his heritage. Proud to be both a Navajo *and* an American, and it was because of Sam that both he and Jackson had their feelings of self-worth and their self-esteem intact.

It hadn't always been that way, at least not for Jackson, who was only half Navajo. The mother who had deserted him had been Caucasian and from what his own mother had told him about the other woman, she had made Jackson feel that his Native American side was what dragged him down.

Jackson had had a lot going against him and to his credit—and Sam's—he had come a long way, Garrett thought. That was part of what he wanted this writer's article to reflect. That Jackson had been the first youthful offender who had been turned around by what he'd learned at the Healing Ranch—even if the ranch hadn't been called that at the time. Back then it had just been a working ranch—and he and Jackson had been the ones doing the working—right alongside their uncle.

These days it was still a working ranch, but its purpose now was a little different from the one it had when Jackson was brought in to work there as a troubled teen.

Damn, how could this woman have gotten lost? Garrett wondered, slowly urging his horse on. The road was fairly straight from Laredo to here. All she had to do was stay on it.

There were no storms anywhere in that stretch of land to divert her, not even one brewing on the horizon, according to the latest weather report, so where the hell was she?

Garrett squinted as he stared out along the road below. Even from here, he should be able to see the dust the car was kicking up.

Okay, so the car was tan and that didn't exactly stand out immediately in this area. If she'd rented a car that was a royal blue, the color that was still pretty popular in the glossy magazine ads he looked at on occasion, she would be easier to spot. But even in a tan car, he felt he could still find her. It was just harder.

But harder didn't mean impossible. It just meant that—

Garrett abruptly stopped giving himself a pep talk and really stared down at the road below him. There was something pulled over to the side.

It was a tan compact car.

Her car, he thought triumphantly. He'd found her, Garrett congratulated himself.

There was no cloud of dust, big or little, coming from around it. Now that he had finally spotted it, he saw that the vehicle wasn't moving.

Why wasn't it moving? he wondered in the next heartbeat. Had she run out of gas, or had the car just died?

And then an even worse thought suddenly occurred to Garrett.

Had the woman passed out for some reason?

With women like his late mother, Sylvia, Miss Joan, the tart-tongued woman with the heart of gold who owned the diner, and now Debi, the nurse who had married his brother, populating his life, he was accustomed to thinking of women as inherently strong. He was used to women like Debi who rolled up her sleeves, went out and got the job done, not women who fainted at the first sign of trouble.

From what he'd managed to gather from the editor he'd talked to, this woman from the magazine might very well fall into the latter group, not the former.

If that was the case, whether she was spooked or had fainted, he had better get down there to her pronto. There was no telling what sort of condition this woman was in—and how that might, ultimately, reflect on the Healing Ranch.

He knew that was a selfish thought, but when it came to Jackson, he could be as selfish as he had to be.

The fastest way from where he was to where she was down below was straight down the hillside. It was the fastest way, but definitely not the easiest.

"You up to this, boy?" he asked, patting his golden palomino's neck.

There was no question that the stallion he had raised from a foal was sure-footed, but he had never actually put Wicked to the test, at least not for more than a couple of feet.

Garrett looked down, undecided. It was a lot more than a couple of feet between where he was and where the woman's car was.

"This is going to be tricky," he said.

The words were intended for him rather than for the horse he regarded as more than just an animal. Wicked and he had a strong bond, and the horse would push himself to the limit for him. That was just the way things were.

At the same time, he didn't want to do anything that just might cause the stallion to injure himself.

"You've got to go nice and slow, a little bit at a time." He spoke in a steady, firm cadence, encouraging the horse. "But you can do it."

Garrett was completely aware that once they started, there was no turning back, no do-overs. They could only continue on the path they were on. But he felt he had no choice, he had to try it. The woman might be hurt, which was probably why she was pulled over like that and if she was hurt, then time was important and going the other roundabout route would take him at least three times as long.

Mentally crossing his fingers and all but holding his breath, Garrett gave Wicked the command to start down the side of the hill. The horse obeyed.

He held on to the reins as tightly as he dared, not wanting to pull the horse back too much because he was afraid that it might cause Wicked to either grow skittish or actually rear back, neither of which would end well for them.

What ultimately resulted was something that, to the casual observer, looked as if the horse was sliding down the hillside in slow motion, his front hooves going first, sending bits and pieces of dirt and a little grass raining down ahead of him. The same, a little less forcefully, was happening with the back hooves.

Progress was slow and careful, but after what felt like an eternity later to Garrett, he and Wicked were on flat ground at the bottom of the hill several feet away from the parked car.

The feeling of relief was almost dizzying. He couldn't help wondering if Wicked felt the same way.

"Extra lumps of sugar for you today when we get back," Garrett promised, leaning over slightly in the saddle in order to pat the horse's neck. Both of them, he noticed, were sweating. He felt more connected to the palomino than ever.

"Hell, extra lumps of sugar for you for a week," Garrett amended. "You could have sent me flying right over your head and breaking my fool neck with just one misstep," he acknowledged with more than a little feeling. "Thanks for not doing that." He took a breath, steadying what he realized was a ragged case of nerves. "Now let's see what's wrong with this tenderfoot," he proposed to his four-footed companion.

Still not knowing what to expect, he guided Wicked closer to the car, then dismounted. With the reins held tightly in one hand, he approached the vehicle slowly, then peered into its interior.

Garrett was still about three feet away from the tan car when the driver's door swung open and a petite woman in tight jeans and what looked like a suede, fringed jacket jumped out like a jack-in-the-box on a delayed timer.

Looking at her, he couldn't decide whether she looked terrified and was attempting to hide it, or if she was braced for a fight but undecided as to how to defend herself.

Pressing her back against the opened driver's side door, the woman shouted at him. "I don't have any money on me!"

"That's okay," he told her, staying put for the moment even as he raised his free hand in a gesture to reassure her. "I wasn't going to ask you for any—and why are you yelling?"

Maybe it was his imagination, but the woman—he had no idea that they made writers so sexy—looked a little chagrined, as well as leery. "So you can hear me."

"I can hear you just fine even if you lowered your voice. As a matter of fact, maybe even better," he amended, trying to get her to smile.

So far, it wasn't working.

Because Kim had absolutely no idea how to defend herself in this sort of a situation, she was forced to make it up as she went along. Why hadn't she thought to pack her can of mace? Did mace even work on a horse if he used the horse to attack her?

Even as she started to talk, it sounded lame to her ear. Despite the fact that she had lived her entire life in San Francisco, she had never been in a situation where she felt threatened. She'd had to come out here for that, she thought grudgingly. She was going to find a way to get even with Saunders if it was the last thing she ever did.

"I'm not alone. I've got people coming," she announced, raising her voice again as if the increased volume would bring these "people" faster—either that or scare him away.

"Are you Kimberly?" he asked, even as he searched his brain for the last name that the editor had told him. The last name that was temporarily eluding him.

And then he remembered.

"Kimberly Lee?" he asked.

The woman's eyes widened even more. He would have found it hypnotic under any other circumstances.

"How do you know my name?" she demanded nervously.

He couldn't get over how adorable she looked. Spooked, most likely feisty if her stance was any indication, but definitely adorable. He began to relax. He could work with adorable. Adorable women were his specialty.

"Well, I could try to dazzle you with a few mysterious answers, tell you my ancestors were into reading minds—" and then he cracked a grin "—but the truth of it is, your editor told me."

The woman eyed him suspiciously. "Miles?" she asked.

"No, that's not the name he gave me. I think he said it was Stan—" Garrett searched his memory again— names were not his long suit. And, just like with her last name, he remembered. Belatedly. "Stan Saunders, that's it."

How could he have forgotten that last name? he upbraided himself. It was the same as one of the boys Jackson had been personally working with. A dark-eyed, defiant kid who had taken more time to get through to than most of the rest.

He caught himself wondering if there was some sort of a connection between the kid and the editor, then decided probably not. Saunders wasn't *that* unusual a name. Most likely it was just a coincidence. Unlike his brother, he believed that there was such a thing as coincidences and moreover, he believed that they happened more than just once in a while.

"You talked to Stan Saunders?" Kim asked, surprised.

Looking at the tall, dark-haired man for the first time—*really* looking at him, she realized that he might be the main man she was supposed to interview. And then again, she wouldn't have been able to actually swear to it. It hadn't been a very good picture, just something she'd managed to find in a local newspaper article.

"What about?" she asked, still suspicious.

"He got worried when he couldn't reach you on your cell phone." Garrett remained where he was. He had a feeling that if he tried to get closer, she just might run. Not that there was anywhere to run to, but he'd still have to catch her and it was too hot for that kind of exertion. "He asked me to find you."

"You're Jackson?" she asked, still a little on her guard but she had to admit that she was feeling less defensive than she'd been a minute ago.

"Garrett," he corrected. "The *other* White Eagle," he added with a touch of humor.

He had a nice smile, she thought. But then, she'd read somewhere that Ted Bundy had a nice smile. Still, she began to relax.

"Well, Garrett-the-other-White-Eagle, you have no cell reception out here," she complained. And then to prove her point, she held up the phone that still wasn't registering a signal.

Garrett nodded. "It's been known to happen on occasion," he acknowledged.

She was right. This was a hellhole. "How long an occasion?" she asked.

The shrug was quick and generally indifferent, as if there were far more important matters to tend to. "It varies." He nodded at her compact. "What's wrong with your car?"

She glanced over her shoulder. "Nothing, I just didn't want to drive it if I didn't know where I was going." A small pout accompanied the next accusation. "I lost the GPS signal."

Garrett took that in stride. Nothing unusual about that either, he supposed, even though neither he nor anyone he knew even had a GPS in their car. They relied far more on their own instincts and general familiarity with the area.

He did move just a little closer now. He saw that she was watching him, as if uncertain whether or not to trust him yet. He could see her side of it. After all, it was just the two of them out here and she only had his word for who he was.

"You can follow me, then," he told her, then added with a smile that was intended to dazzle her—several of Miss Joan's waitresses had told him his smile was one of his best features, "Consider me your guiding light."

You're cute, no doubt about that, but I'll hold off on the whole guiding-light thing, if you don't mind, Kim thought.

She stifled a sigh as she got in behind the wheel of her car. She *knew* she should have dug in and fought getting stuck with this assignment.

Chapter Three

Well, Kim thought wryly, following close behind Garrett, she had to admit that this was certainly different. She was definitely *not* accustomed to being treated to the rear view of a horse.

Granted, Garrett created a rather intriguing, captivating specimen of manhood, sitting atop his horse the way he was, but she hadn't come here to stare at the back of some man, muscular and impressive though he might appear to be.

Garrett White Eagle—if that was who he really was and she had only his word for that—seemed nice enough, but for all she knew, that engaging smile of his could be hiding the soul of a sadist.

A sadist who lured trusting women off to some obscure hideaway where no one would ever find them—or her—until years later.

A hideaway in a hole-in-the-wall. Now there was irony for you. Maybe she should flee now while she still could.

Kim's hands tightened on the steering wheel and she was all set to execute a U-turn and make her getaway when she saw it.

A ranch house in the distance.

So there really *was* a ranch out here. Maybe this was actually all on the level after all, which meant that Garrett White Eagle actually *was* Garrett White Eagle, just as he claimed to be.

Kim's relief at spotting the ranch—civilization at last—was rather short-lived when she took a closer look at the actual structure she was driving toward.

Garrett turned around just then, as he had been doing every couple of minutes to make sure that she was still following him.

"Something wrong?" Garrett asked, pulling up on Wicked's reins.

Even though he was leading the way and going so slowly he was afraid Wicked would fall asleep in mid-step, the woman didn't exactly fill him with confidence about her navigational skills.

He saw the stunned expression on Kim's face. Her mouth had all but dropped open.

Now what?

When her eyes shifted toward him, he saw the confusion in them.

"Where's the main house?" she asked, then said, "That's the cook's quarters, right?"

Garrett inclined his head, as if in agreement. "Uh-huh. The cook's quarters, the main ranch hand's quarters, Jackson's quarters—along with his wife, Debi—and, oh yes, my quarters, too."

"All of you live there?" she asked, as if the concept hadn't quite sunk in.

"Uh-huh." His eyes never left her face.

Kim's eyes widened as her driving definitely slowed down to almost a crawl. It was as if her little car had gone on automatic pilot and was now driving itself.

She chewed on her lower lip before asking, "That's the main house?" If she was trying to hide the appalled note in her voice, she was failing.

He had to admit, after having talked to her for a couple of minutes, her reaction didn't come as much of a surprise.

Garrett laughed. "Let me guess, you were expecting South Fork."

Her eyebrows knitted together, as she struggled to hide her disappointment over the building she saw. "South Fork?" she echoed. "What's that?"

"Something obviously before your time," he told her. Then, not wanting to seem old in her eyes, he added, "Before mine, too. Except that I like watching old, classic TV programs. To answer your question, South Fork was this big, sprawling fictional ranch just outside of Dallas that belonged to this really rich family whose members were always arguing and at each other's throats all the time. But I've got to admit, the ranch house they had was a thing of beauty," he told her. "This might not be South Fork," he allowed, "but it's all ours."

There was no missing the pride in his voice.

To each his own, Kim thought, stifling the urge to shrug at his response. If that ranch house up ahead had been hers, she would have done whatever she needed to in order to make it look better in a hurry—and then she would have sold it as fast as she could before the buyer could think twice about the wisdom of getting stuck with a rundown house and a ranch that wasn't producing much of anything except work.

As if reading her mind, Garrett leaned down from his horse and promised, "It'll grow on you."

She wasn't going to be here long enough for that to happen, but for now, she kept that fact to herself.

Before she'd left, she had told Stan that she would write the best article she could on the Healing Ranch, but after seeing the place, she estimated it shouldn't take her more than a day to whip up her article. Two if she deliberately stalled and didn't get started for the first day.

And since she wanted to get out of Prairie Gulch as fast as she could, she would get started as fast as she could.

Kim prided herself on knowing how to put someone at ease so that they would confide in her.

Looking at the house as she drew closer, she promised herself to "make nice" with the people out here, get her story—or rather Stan's story since he was the one who was so keen on it, not her—and then get back home. If she were particularly diligent, she'd be back in time to hand Stan her copy and then go shopping at Barneys, the New York–based department store that had found a second home in San Francisco and had become one of her treasured stomping grounds of choice.

With that in mind, Kim turned up her smile several watts and told her guide in the sweetest voice possible, "I think it's charming."

Garrett laughed, not taken in for a second, although he had to admit she was the prettiest liar he'd ever had to deal with.

"No, you don't," he contradicted. "But that's okay, it's not supposed to be 'charming.' It's supposed to be functional. And it is. This is where the 'bad' boys get sent in order to be turned into human beings, something that my brother, Jackson, does, time and again, very, very well."

"And you? What do you do?" she asked. She'd stopped driving for a moment and was taking in the ranch in its entirety.

Did it get any less run-down from close up? She certainly hoped so. She was planning on taking a few photographs to go with her article and right now, she didn't see a good angle to use for her shots of the ranch house's exterior.

"Anything I have to," Garrett said in response, his voice dropping by an octave or so. Enough to get her attention and have her wondering things that wouldn't be finding their way into the article.

"Define 'anything,'" she requested in a mildly intrigued voice.

"Just what it sounds like," he replied, looking at her and punctuating his answer with a wink that seemed to flutter directly down into her stomach, causing just the slightest mini–tidal wave to take place there.

Kim paused to take in a discreet breath before continuing. The breath was to help steady her unexpected reaction to this dusty cowboy who fancied himself a ladies' man.

"I'll pin you down for details later," she told him. "Right now, I'd like to meet your brother before I go into town to see about my hotel reservation." She glanced at her watch before continuing to drive toward the ranch house. "I'm already running late," she realized. "How long will they hold a room at the hotel?"

Garrett had to struggle to keep the laugh from surfacing. The hotel wasn't exactly beating off patrons with a stick.

"As long as it takes," he finally replied. The corners of his mouth curved despite his best efforts to keep a straight, if not dour face.

She wondered if everyone in this quaint little dust bowl of a town talked in circles. Just what was he telling her about her hotel room? "I don't think I understand."

"We don't exactly have a lot of tourists coming through Forever," he told her. "There's no danger of losing your room to someone else, not unless a twister suddenly comes through, taking down every building except for the hotel. That happens, *then* you might have to be concerned about losing your room to someone else if they get there first. But until then, I wouldn't worry about it if I were you. You're in the driver's seat, trust me."

That didn't make any sense to her. "If that's the case, how does the hotel stay in business?"

"Good question," he acknowledged. Kim struggled not to feel resentful, as if she was being patronized. "The hotel belongs to this construction company that sees it as getting some sort of a toehold in the region," he went on to explain. "The owner's not in it for the money," he confided. "The way matters had turned out, the general contractor wound up owning the building— and she'd married Finn Murphy, so her stake in building up the town has definitely gone up."

"That doesn't seem possible," Kim told him, certain that Garrett was making this all up, trying to pull the wool over the outsider's eyes with this tall tale. Who wasn't in it for the money? If not that, then they were in it for the prestige, the way her parents were. And this was definitely *not* a place someone came in order to build up their reputation.

Just how naive did this man think she was?

Did she come across as naive? Kim caught herself suddenly wondering.

That was *not* the image she was going for. Smart, sassy, capable, *those* were the buzz words she was after, not *naive*.

"A lot of things in Forever and the places around it don't really seem possible," Garrett informed her. "Forever isn't exactly your run-of-the-mill kind of place."

"Oh, God, just like Brigadoon," Kim murmured under her breath before she could think better of it and stop herself.

Garrett had overheard her despite the fact that she had meant the comment only for herself, but the reference went right over his head.

"Like what?" he asked, looking at her quizzically.

A strapping he-man like Garrett White Eagle undoubtedly thought all musicals were products of stupid, self-involved minds. She wasn't about to give him ammunition to use against her. This job was going to be hard enough as it was. She wanted to be taken seriously—even by this cowboy.

"Never mind," Kim said dismissively. "It's not a real place, anyway."

Garrett had absolutely no idea what she was talking about, but he felt it wasn't really polite to tell her that. So, at least for now, he just let Kim's remark slide.

"Well, Forever's real, all right," he assured her. "It's just different."

She took a deep breath, more than a little relieved to be able to distance herself from the subject. "I'm beginning to see that," she replied.

She drove the rest of the short distance to the ranch

house and got out of her car. Garrett dismounted almost parallel to her vehicle and let the palomino's reins drop to the ground in front of him.

Walking away from Wicked, he stepped onto the front porch.

Kim looked at his horse uncertainly. She fully expected to be trampled any second if the horse got it into his head that she was standing in his way, blocking his access to something.

"Aren't you going to tie him up?" she asked, shifting closer to Garrett.

She was banking on him protecting her if the horse suddenly went rogue—or whatever it was called when horses charged at people for no reason.

"Wicked's not into bondage," Garrett told her with a grin.

The cowboy was making fun of her because she was clearly out of her element, she thought. Since she needed his help—at least for the moment—she did her best not to act offended.

Instead, she told herself to try harder to get on this cowboy's good side. The faster she got this story down, the faster she'd be back in San Francisco, mistress of her own fate—with her rent paid.

"No, I mean won't your horse take off if you don't tie his reins to something?" she pointed out.

"Not unless you plan to scare him," Garrett said with a laugh. And then he answered her question more seriously. "Wicked's trained to stay wherever I put down his reins. He knows not to run off," he told her. "That comes in handy when we're out on the range and there's nothing to tie him to."

Kim glanced from the horse to his rider. She wouldn't

have known how to begin to train an animal for something like that—which was why, among other reasons, she'd never gotten a pet.

"That's pretty clever," she said honestly.

"Wicked's pretty clever," Garrett corrected, giving the animal he had trained the credit he felt the stallion deserved.

While he regarded animals to be smarter than a lot of people realized, he was aware that, like people, some animals were smarter than others. In his estimation, Wicked was exceedingly smart.

"Be right back," Garrett told her, going inside the house.

"Okay," Kim said cheerfully. The man was modest. Getting on his good side with flattery was going to be harder than she thought, but she was determined to do it. If she could get him to open up, she was confident that all the details she needed for this article would just come pouring out of him and the story would wind up writing itself.

Twenty-four hours and she was going to be out of here, she promised herself.

Thirty-six at the most.

Life with two overachieving parents and two overachieving sisters had taught her to hedge her bets—up to a point. Although, from what she could see, there wasn't anything to write about here that could possibly keep her for even as long as a whole day, could it? she wondered. The brothers had a ranch, they worked with so-called troubled kids and they had some horses around. End of story. The challenge would be to flesh all that out to even a minimum length of words.

Kim frowned to herself. She doubted that *anyone*

would want to read what she'd just outlined in her head. There *had* to be some kind of an angle she could use to at least make this article somewhat interesting instead of the snooze-fest it was shaping up to be.

"Jackson's not here," Garrett told her as he came out of the house a couple of minutes after he'd gone in. "He's probably at the corral, still working with the boys."

"Okay." Turning around on her heel, she left the porch and headed toward her vehicle again.

Instead of following her, Garrett remained where he was—on the porch—and watched her. When he saw her opening the door on the driver's side, he asked, "What are you doing?"

"I'm getting into the car."

"Why?"

Maybe she'd misjudged the man's mental acuity. He certainly hadn't struck her as being slow, but what other explanation could there be for his not understanding what she was telling him?

"So I can drive to the corral." He wasn't picking up his horse's reins. Why? "You are going to lead the way on your horse, right?"

Instead of taking Wicked's reins, he came around to her side of the vehicle.

"You don't need the car," he told her, shutting the door for her. "We'll walk."

"Walk?" Kim echoed in surprise, as if she was unable to fully grasp the concept.

"Walk," he repeated gently, taking her hand in his and fully intending to coax her along if he had to. "It's what people do when they put one foot in front of the other." He grinned. "You'd be amazed at how much ground you can cover that way."

Kim was hardly listening to him. Instead, she looked around the immediate surrounding area. She didn't see anything beside the ranch house.

"Just how far away is the corral?" she asked.

Amusement highlighted his eyes, but he managed to keep a straight face as he replied, "Close enough not to have to take a canteen with us."

The straight face didn't fool her for a second. This time, she called him on it. "You're making fun of me, aren't you?"

"I wouldn't dream of it," he told her innocently, then added, "I might, however, be teasing you a little." In the next breath, he apologized. "Sorry, I don't get to have much fun. Working with Jackson and a bunch of boys can get pretty serious at times and I don't get into town much."

She sincerely doubted that. She might not know much about ranches and towns in the middle of no-where, but she felt she was pretty good when it came to judging people, and Garrett White Eagle did *not* strike her as a man who was resigned to living some sort of a monastic life. He looked, instead, like a man who knew how to have a good time.

He also struck her as someone who knew how to read people and work an angle.

This ranch, it suddenly occurred to her now that she wasn't distracted, cursing at defunct Wi-Fi signals and guidance systems that refused to guide, could be a per-fect source of income. Parents were known to become desperate when it came to trying to save an offspring who was on the road to self-destruction. One that would bring them everlasting shame, not to mention huge law-yer fees and who knew what all else if those kids re-ally got going. And then one day, they hear about this supposedly altruistic place that promises to heal their wayward liability, turn him into a pillar of society for what they were probably told would be a "reasonable" sum of money.

Who wouldn't be sucked into taking a chance on that? Especially when rehabs were notorious for their rate of turning out repeat violators.

An article like that could almost write itself, she thought as she all but trotted next to Garrett, doing her best to keep up.

But why bother when Garrett could practically write it for her? Or, at the very least, give her the lead she wanted to go with.

"Just how much can you and your brother pad the bills for these boys without arousing the parents' sus-picions?" she asked, almost sounding breathless as the question came out of her mouth.

Garrett stopped dead in his tracks just shy of the cor-ral. Had he just heard what he *thought* he just heard? Be-cause, if he had, the last thing he needed or wanted was for Jackson to get wind of this writer's current mind-set.

He needed to change her mind, fast—or, barring that, he needed to send her on her way.

Also fast.

Chapter Four

Garrett wasn't about to take another step until he got this cleared up.

If Jackson even caught a hint about what this woman was mistakenly thinking regarding the Healing Ranch's bottom line, the interview—and any business resulting from it—would be totally dead in the water, especially since Jackson hadn't been keen on having someone do an in-depth article on the ranch in the first place.

Garrett approached denial carefully, knowing that if he was heated in expressing his feelings, Kim was bound to think there was a story buried here.

"I don't think you have the right idea about what we do here," he told her.

Kim had given up believing in an altruistic world a long time ago—probably somewhere around the time she went into kindergarten, thanks to her older sisters who had made sure that she knew there was no Santa Claus, no magical elf who gave for the sake of giving.

Kim believed that everyone, no matter who they were, wanted to get ahead. That didn't necessarily make it a bad thing. After all, money was what made the world go around. Wasn't she here, doing a story that held no interest for her and was nothing more than a puff piece, just because she needed to pay the rent?

"From what I'm told by my editor—who's very high on this place, by the way—you and your brother do a really good job with these troubled teens, so why shouldn't you be compensated?"

"There's a difference between 'compensated' and the word you used. 'Padded' has a whole different meaning attached to it," he pointed out.

She hadn't meant to insult him. If anything she admired the White Eagles for what they did. They were good at something and they were making it pay off while helping kids out, as well. It seemed like a win-win situation from where she stood. Why did this cowboy look as if she was guilty of throwing rocks at his brother and him?

"Look, no offense intended, Garrett," she told him. "But this all can't be strictly charitable work that's happening here. After all, you've got to be able to survive. No one's going to fault you for that," she assured him.

Garrett took a breath. He had to find a way to set her straight and make her understand. "We don't do it for free—"

"That's all I'm saying—"

Garrett shook his head. He still didn't think she understood what Jackson was doing here. "That's not what I'm hearing, though," he said. "The parents, or guardians if there're no parents in the picture, are charged for the teen's room and board."

"What else?" Kim prodded.

"There is no 'else,'" Garrett told her. He hadn't thought she was jaded, but he'd obviously misjudged her. "I see where you're going with this and in this case, you're on the wrong path." He didn't want her thinking he was being preachy or coming off holier-than-thou. He had a feeling she'd skewer him, Jackson *and* the ranch if that was the impression she came away with.

"Not that I didn't try to get Jackson to charge a little more just so we could get ahead of the game—and by 'ahead' I mean get a little money put aside for the low periods so we could keep the place open even if there aren't enough teens here needing to be set straight for us to cover the bills."

He paused, trying to choose his words well. If he couldn't get through to her, from his point of view there would be no reason to continue this interview—but he had a feeling she'd still write a piece and it just might not be the kind he was hoping for—and Jackson would really have a reason to be angry.

That meant he *had* to get her to understand what they—especially Jackson—were doing here.

"Right now, we're in the red, which is why I talked Jackson into agreeing to let you do this story."

"Wait, he doesn't want me writing about what you're doing here at the Healing Ranch?" Kim asked, surprised. She assumed that everyone wanted free publicity. The only people who didn't had something to hide.

"Jackson's very private and he didn't want any of the boys put under a microscope, either," he explained. "I was the one who talked him into it because I was hoping that the exposure might make more people aware of the ranch's existence. I figure that the more people know, the more people might want to send their kids here. And that way, we get to stay on top of our bills instead of one step ahead of foreclosure."

She would have to do more research to find out just

how much of what Garrett had just said was actually true. He certainly seemed sincere enough—but so did the most successful con artists. Just because Garrett was ruggedly handsome with soulful eyes didn't make him honest or selfless.

She played devil's advocate. "That sounds very melo-dramatic," she told him.

Garrett shrugged and she found herself captivated by the way his broad shoulders rose and fell.

"It's also very true—not that that's something Jackson wants made public, either," he warned. "I'm only telling you this so that you drop the notion that my brother is lining his pockets with the extorted money of worried-sick parents. The charges vary and depend on how long the kid stays. As for those parents who can't afford to pay for the Healing Ranch but whose kid really needs to come to a place like this, Jackson lets them make payment schedules they can live with."

He could see that the woman was still somewhat skeptical. He knew it was against Jackson's rules, but he gave her an example to back up what he was saying, omitting only the people's actual names.

"One family's kid was here when he was twelve—a real hellion, by the way. He's about to graduate high school this coming June—and they're still making pay-ments."

"He charged them that much?" Kim asked, stunned.

"No." Was the woman baiting him? Garrett won-dered. "Jackson made the payments that small—after giving them a discount. The kid's father was a wounded vet, his mother was an elementary school teacher. They had two more kids at home." There were times when his brother exasperated him, but he had to admit that when the dust finally settled, he was nothing if not damn proud of Jackson. "I'm the greedy one in the family— Jackson remembers his roots."

She waited a beat and when Garrett didn't say anything to fill her in, she asked, "And those roots are—?"

"—for him to tell you about." Jackson would be the best judge on how much he wanted to let the woman know, Garrett thought. "I've already done too much talking," he told her.

In her view, there was no such thing as too much talking. "I thought this was both your stories," she pointed out, trying to flatter Garrett. In her experience, people always talked as long as they felt they had a friendly audience.

Garrett, apparently, would be the exception that proved the rule.

"No," he contradicted. "It's Jackson's story. I'm just along for the ride."

Kim frowned slightly. She sincerely doubted that. From what Stan had told her, it seemed as if both brothers ran this ranch and shared equally in the work it took to oversee anywhere between four to ten teenaged boys at a time. At least half, she assumed, were really problematic.

Garrett began walking again. She fell into place beside him.

"Why boys?" she asked suddenly just before they approached the corral.

The question had come out of the blue without any connection to what she'd asked last. It caught him off guard. "Excuse me?"

"Why boys?" Kim repeated. This question she intended to get an honest answer to, no matter how much he danced around it. "You only have boys here. Why not girls, too?" She watched his face closely as she went on. "Or don't you and your brother consider girls worth helping?"

If he didn't feel that there was a lot riding on this, he would have been amused at the dogged way she kept trying to unearth something less than flattering about the way the ranch was run. But there *was* a lot riding on this, so he wanted her to get it right.

"It's not like that," he told her, then offered a speculation as he continued, "I suppose that there are more boys who get in trouble than girls—"

"Or maybe the girls just don't get caught."

"Maybe," Garrett allowed. "It might also be that it's easier working with boys if they're not distracted," he pointed out, "and girls can be a really huge distraction to guys."

The way he said it, looking deep into her eyes, suddenly had her pulse racing.

I bet you're really something else when you get going, aren't you, Garrett White Eagle? she thought, doing her best to get her breathing back under control. For a second it had felt as if the very air had just backed up in her lungs and then *stayed* there.

"Is that what you think?" Kim asked him when she finally found her tongue. "That girls are a huge distraction?"

"I don't 'think,'" Garrett retorted, then added, "I know."

His face, when he leaned over her like that, was just inches away from hers and for one moment, she thought he was going to follow through on what she was certain was on his mind. He was going to kiss her and she had to admit that she didn't exactly find the prospect off-putting.

But the next moment, the whimsical smile was back on his lips again as he straightened up, putting distance between their faces—and her sanity returned. Getting physically involved with the subject of her article—or at least *one* of the subjects—was definitely a bad idea.

Even though he was awfully appealing.

"Why don't I introduce you to my brother?" he was suggesting as her mind did cartwheels off in the corner somewhere.

When he looked at her like that, she found that she actually had to summon up saliva in order to say anything in response—the inside of her mouth had gone that dry.

"Why don't you?" she agreed, doing her best not to croak out the words.

C'mon, Kim, get a grip, she told herself sternly, doing her best to focus on what had brought her here in the first place—she was doing a story that would allow her to pay her rent. Getting distracted was no way to become a celebrated writer—or even build a reputation that would amount to a hill of beans.

All she was trying to do now was keep the wolf from the door.

It occurred to her, as the thought flashed through her mind, that she had something in common with Jackson White Eagle after all.

At that point, they had reached the corral and she was acutely aware that everyone—with the exception of the tall, dark-haired cowboy in the center, the man she took to be Garrett's older brother—had stopped what they were doing and turned to look at her.

While she was accustomed to covert attention—even liked it—blatant attention was something new, especially when it came from those who couldn't vote yet.

"Why are they all staring?" she asked Garrett in what she hoped was a really low whisper.

Garrett grinned as he spared her a longer-than-necessary look. "Off hand, I could think of several reasons, none of which I can share with you without risking getting slapped."

She laughed shortly and shook her head. "Is that your idea of a compliment?"

"No," he replied with a deliberately innocent expression, "that's my idea of the truth."

She took a quick inventory of the teens in the corral. While most looked respectfully polite, none of them looked as if they were even remotely naive or backward. Just what kind of bill of goods was Garrett trying to sell her?

"You're telling me that these boys aren't used to women?" It wasn't so much a question as an accusation.

"No, but with the possible exception of my sister-in-law, I'd say that they're definitely not used to women who look like you."

"Eurasian?" she guessed. Kim was well aware that in a backwoodsy place like this, she didn't exactly blend in with the local population for obvious reasons.

"Actually, I was thinking more along the lines of the word *gorgeous*," he told her.

This one was a smooth operator who used his charm to get by, Kim thought. "Emphasis on the word *line*."

"Well, if we're going to be emphasizing words, in this case I'd zero in on the word *truth*," he told her with the same casual air he might have employed rattling off all the merits of his favorite beer.

Casual, but at the same time, loaded. The man was single-handedly raising the immediate temperature around her. He was definitely smooth. As smooth as any so-called stud she might have encountered in one of the upscale watering holes or restaurants in San Francisco.

"What are you doing in a place like this?" she asked him honestly. He was the type she would have figured would be chomping at the bit to get out of town and the first one to take off the moment his high school diploma hit his hand.

"Helping my brother," Garrett answered without a moment's hesitation. His eyes met hers and she could feel her stomach tighten just a sliver. "I thought you already knew that."

"I was filled in," Kim acknowledged. "But there's a difference between being told something and understanding why."

"Nothing to understand," Garrett assured her as Jackson, finally finished with instructing one of his "hands," as he referred to the teens, approached them. "This ranch saved my brother's life and when he wanted to return the favor, or rather, pass it on, he asked me to help him. There was no way I would have ever turned my back on that."

"So you're the loyal type." In her family, it was competition rather than loyalty that ruled. At least, between her sisters—and possibly her parents, as well. She was the one on the outside, the one who merited their pity and just maybe her sisters' smug superiority.

"Something like that," Garrett allowed.

The next moment, he took the opportunity to table

this uncomfortable discussion and did the honors of introducing his brother to the woman he had convinced Jackson should come here.

As he handled the introductions, Garrett mentally crossed his fingers and prayed he wasn't going to regret this.

And that Jackson wouldn't wind up holding it against him.

"Jackson," he smiled broadly at his older brother, "this is Kimberly Lee. She's the writer that *Western Times Magazine* sent to write about our work here at the Healing Ranch."

Jackson, Kim immediately noted, was as tall and as handsome as his younger brother. His face was a little leaner and his cheekbones were a bit more prominent, but their hair was equally sleek and black and their eyes were both a surprising, intense, remarkable shade of blue.

Jackson's build, she also noticed, was a tad more sinewy while Garrett's was more muscular. But anyone looking at them could immediately see that they were brothers.

Was that what ultimately tied them together? she wondered. Their Native American heritage? Or was it something that went deeper than that?

She supposed the answer to that question might very well be part of the story she was doing on them. She was going to need another angle, seeing as how the monetary one was now off the table—if she believed Garrett, which, until it was proven otherwise, she did.

After a moment, as if against his will and own better judgment, Jackson leaned slightly forward and put out his hand.

She could almost *see* his reluctance. Was he just exceedingly modest—or was there some other, possibly more nefarious reason for the man's aw-shucks behavior?

"Welcome to the Healing Ranch, Miss Lee," Jackson said.

"Thank you," she said, forcing a wide smile to her lips as she shook his hand. The next second she was taken with the strength of his grip. Most men would shake her hand as if they were touching a sparrow, obviously thinking of her as too fragile to endure a normal handshake. Jackson had paid her the compliment of treating her like an equal, a person. She looked at him with new respect. "Was that your idea?" she asked.

Jackson blinked. "Excuse me?"

God, but these brothers were polite. Was that genuine, or just for show so that she came away with a favorable impression of them? She was beginning to think that just maybe it was the former. But the jury wasn't totally back yet.

"The name of this place. The Healing Ranch. Was that your idea or your brother's?" she asked, glancing at Garrett before continuing. "Or was the name already in place when you took over?"

Jackson paused for a moment, as if trying to remember. But then he shrugged. "I guess it was mine. Look, I don't mean to be rude, but I'm running a little behind today. Besides, I'm not really good at this sort of thing." Putting a hand on his brother's shoulder, he all but pushed him forward. "Garrett's going to be your guide. If you have any questions about the ranch or anything that we do here, he's your man. Garrett's got a better memory than I do, anyway. So, if you'll excuse me," Jackson said, already backing away.

But she wasn't about to just be handed off—although she had to admit that she'd had worse offers tendered to her.

Kim raised her voice to be heard as Jackson was putting distance between them. "I will have some questions for you."

"Garrett can answer anything that I can," Jackson assured her, turning away.

"I'd still like to interview you and have a private conversation—my editor would insist on it," she added, rising up on her toes as if that would help her voice to carry to him.

She didn't really know if Stan would care about the one-on-one interview as much as he would care that she got all the spellings right and put down the general gist of the story to the best of her knowledge and ability. Stan cared about the facts and about pulling in an audience. Most of all, she knew that Stan liked it when an audience was moved.

If she approached the article the right way, this could be a "feel good" story.

Which meant that if there ultimately *was* a conniving angle to be unearthed, she realized that she was going to have to bury it.

She wouldn't be going for a Pulitzer, Kim thought. Like it or not, what she was really trying to go for was a hanky. One way or another, she was still going to be paid the same amount of money—and ultimately, it was easier writing for a hanky than a Pulitzer.

All she had to do was look for a purely emotional angle. The thought didn't make her happy, but she could do it.

"When I get a chance," Jackson promised, stopping one last time to look back in her direction before re-joining the boys.

Kim turned to look at Garrett. "I guess that just leaves you and me, then," she said, putting on her best thousand-watt smile and aiming it directly at him.

Garrett returned it in spades, unintentionally creating an earthquake in her world.

Maybe this was going to be harder than she thought, Kim decided—and then again, maybe not.

Chapter Five

"C'mon, I'll give you a tour of the ranch," Garrett offered.

Since writing about the Healing Ranch was, after all, why she was here, he just assumed that she would say yes, so he automatically took her arm, leading her away from the corral.

But Kim wasn't all that ready to just fall into step next to him.

"On foot?" she asked incredulously.

From what she'd seen, this was a *big* ranch, and while she was probably in better shape than a lot of people— she believed in doing something with her gym membership other than just keeping the membership card in her wallet—she was *not* up to walking around the entire ranch.

Garrett laughed and dropped his hand from her arm.

"Not the whole thing. I thought you might want to see the stables and the bunkhouse." But that didn't have to be right now if she wanted to come back later. Maybe he should nail down her schedule first, he decided. "How long are you planning on staying?"

She thought for a moment. "I guess that I don't have to check into the hotel room for at least a couple of hours or so."

He hadn't expected her to take him so literally. "No, I mean how long are you planning on staying in Forever in order to write the story?"

As short a time as possible, she thought to herself.

"I'm going to stay as long as it takes to do the story justice." Then, because that sounded a little too naive, she added a realistic coda. "My editor's earmarked the article for the February 1st issue, but if I wind up taking longer to nail down all the details and get them right, then it'll go into the February 15th issue."

There, that should make him think that she was taking her time with this article, Kim thought.

"Why?" she asked abruptly when another reason for his question occurred to her. "Do you want me gone in a certain amount of time?"

"Not me," Garrett told her, a whimsical smile playing on his lips. "I'd be happy to have you stay here for as long as you want."

Kim ignored the warm feeling that washed over her. Instead, she read between the lines of what he was saying. "But your brother does."

"I wouldn't exactly say that, but strangers aren't his thing," Garrett explained with a vague, dismissive shrug.

"Then he must *really* be uncomfortable most of the time. Why would he *do* what he does if he's not comfortable around strangers?" she asked. "That's all he deals with, right?"

He'd have to choose his words carefully around this woman. Well, he supposed that no situation was perfect and this story would give them the boost they needed to reach a wider base. They needed *something* to keep this place open.

"Let me rephrase that," Garrett suggested. "Jackson's not exactly comfortable around most strangers, but that doesn't include these boys. He relates to them, sees himself as *one* of them. You know, 'there but for the grace of God go I' kind of thing," Garrett told her as he took her elbow again.

This time, Kim allowed herself to be led away. But she glanced over her shoulder toward the corral one last time. Jackson was in the middle of a number of teenagers. He was telling them something and they all seemed to be listening to every word as if he was their chosen leader. Not a bored face in the bunch, she noted.

She turned back around to face Garrett. "You know, I *am* going to have to talk to him at one point. Something a little longer than 'hello' and 'goodbye.'"

"Don't worry, you will," Garrett assured her. "It'll be easier when he'll get used to the idea of you being around."

Not going to be here that long, trust me, she thought even as she flashed her widest smile at Garrett.

"I'll just need him to answer a few questions, give me his side of things."

"There aren't any 'sides,'" he told her, thinking that her choice of words was rather odd. "Jackson's not very talkative, but this isn't like a trial or better yet, a mystery, where there are different takes on the way something happened. You're not going to find any deep, hidden reasons for why Jackson started this place if that's what you're looking for."

"All I'm looking for is how the Healing Ranch came to be, the success rate—"

"That's easy enough," he told her. They'd reached

the stable and he held the door open for her, waiting for Kim to walk in first. "It's a hundred percent."

"A hundred percent," she repeated. Was he serious?

"That's right. A hundred percent."

For a moment, she remained standing where she was, just outside the stable. How could he lie like that to her face?

She gave him another chance to pare down the numbers to something more realistic—and truthful. "Every kid who's come here has gone on to be an upstanding citizen, no relapses, no further run-ins with the law?"

Garrett appeared no closer to retracting his statement than he had been a minute ago. "That's what a hundred percent means."

"Wow." The cowboy had nerve, she'd give him that. A whopper of a lie and he didn't even blink an eye. She made a mental note to do some real digging once she got her hands on the list of teens that had spent time here. "That's pretty impressive."

"Jackson doesn't like to brag, so I do it for him," Garrett told her.

Maybe a little too much, she couldn't help thinking. "So what's the magic formula?" she asked Garrett. "How does he—how do you both—go about accomplishing this little miracle?"

She was being sarcastic, but he pretended as if it was a legitimate question and asked her one of his own. "They didn't tell you anything?"

Kim's vague shrug didn't answer his question one way or another—and neither did she.

"Let's just say that I want to hear it from you—and you can start from the beginning," she added.

She was still standing just outside the stable. Garrett wondered if that was on purpose or if she was just unaware of the fact that she'd stopped dead right there.

Garrett had his suspicions.

"You know, it's okay to walk in," he told her. "The stable's not that scary a place."

She wrinkled her nose slightly even before she turned her head toward the interior. "I'm not afraid of it," she said, "I just figured it wouldn't exactly smell too pleasing."

"That only happens if the hands don't get a chance to clean out the stalls," he told her.

The information surprised her—and caused things to fall into place for her. "You have them cleaning out the stables?"

He nodded. "Every morning."

It all made sense now. Just for a second, she'd actually debated buying into the whole altruistic thing. She should have known better.

"So you and your brother make use of the free labor you have on hand."

Damn, this watching what he said really took some doing, Garrett thought, upbraiding his temporary lapse. "I think you might have the wrong take on that."

Kim raised her chin ever so slightly and it made him think of one of the teens who had been among the first to come here. Dwayne Layne had been short for his age and given that and his name—which he later confessed had been used to taunt him with—he was ready to fight if someone so much as looked at him the wrong way. He'd been quite a challenge—and worth every minute of it for the way he'd eventually turned out.

"Then set me straight," Kim was saying.

The woman was smiling as she said it, but he knew

she was issuing a challenge. One he knew he could easily face.

"First of all, it builds character," he told her, once again gently taking hold of her arm. As he talked, he ushered her into the stable, finally getting her in all the way. "They come here, angry and resentful—and yeah, scared," he added, "although they'd rather die than admit it."

"Scared of what?" she asked. "Jackson and you? The other boys?"

"It's simpler than that. They're scared that they're in over their heads, scared that they won't be up to whatever challenges they'll be facing here—scared of looking like fools and being ridiculed by the others—none of which happens, by the way," Garrett emphasized in case she thought that he and Jackson used those kinds of tactics.

The reporter in her who yearned to sink her teeth into a story that mattered, who saw the dark side instead of the light, was highly skeptical of the protest he'd just issued.

"So you say."

He was beginning to expect as much. "You're free to question anyone here—or in Forever," he added, hoping that when—not if—she did, that would finally convince her how they operated this place. "Neither Jackson nor anyone else working here believes in intimidating the boys who are sent here. Granted, they have to be broken down before they're built up again—" he went on.

Kim was quick to point out the discrepancy. "So you do admit that—"

"We break down their bad habits, *not* them. You

don't bring out the good in people by demoralizing them," he told her with feeling.

His passion was almost mesmerizing—but she couldn't allow it to mislead her. "That's very impressive," she told him.

She would need more convincing than he'd first thought, he realized. When he'd initially tried to get someone interested in writing about the Healing Ranch, he'd thought it would be easy and that it would all be good. Apparently, nothing was easy. But then, he'd always liked a challenge.

Especially when it came wrapped up in a beautiful woman.

"It's also very true," he replied simply. "By the way," he went on to point out, "you've stopped wrinkling your nose."

It hadn't occurred to her that she'd stopped until he pointed it out. Taking a subtle deep breath, she noticed that the air was as normal in here as it was outside. No reason not to let him win this round. This way, his guard would be down when she actually did hone in on something.

"I guess your charges actually do a fairly decent job," she acknowledged.

"Yes, they do." Then, not to make them out to be plaster saints, he added, "They're the first ones to reap the rewards of doing it right—and probably the horses like it, too. By the way, Jackson refers to them as ranch hands. It gives them a sense of identity, of their place in the scheme of things here," he explained.

"Ranch hands," she repeated, walking around the stable. All the stalls were empty. She wondered if the horses had been cleared out of here on purpose. Was that because of her? Because he was afraid she might discover something? "I guess that sounds better than free laborers."

"About that," Garrett began.

"Yes?"

"They get paid."

Sure they did. Just how naive did this cowboy think she was?

"Your brother pays them," she said, not buying into what he was attempting to sell her for a second. Her voice stopped just short of mocking what he was telling her.

Garrett nodded as if he didn't realize that she thought he was fabricating everything. "Each job has a different pay range attached to it."

"Pay range?" she questioned.

"If they refuse to do anything, they get nothing," he told her simply, then went into describing the way payments were decided. "They do an unacceptable job, they still get something, but not very much. A good job earns them more and if the job they do is over and above the norm, they get even more than that."

She still found the whole thing doubtful, even though he seemed very sincere as he was reciting all this. "Monopoly money?" she guessed.

"No, it's real money," he assured her. Then, when he saw her raise a brow, he added, "They use it to pay for things here."

"Oh, like a company store," she said, the light suddenly dawning on her. She should have known it was heading in that direction. "How is that not enslaving them?"

Garrett doggedly pushed on. He had no other way to get through to her. "It's done to teach them the value of hard work," he told her. "We don't keep them chained up and starved if they don't work. They just don't have the same range of choices that's opened to them if they do work."

He still hadn't convinced her, but she was beginning to waver just the slightest bit. For the sake of argument, she continued as if she believed him.

"What else do you have them doing other than keeping the stables from smelling like a barn?"

The way she phrased her question had him biting his tongue not to laugh. He knew she wouldn't appreciate thinking that he was having fun at her expense, but her analogy *was* amusing to him.

Composing himself, Garrett answered her question seriously. "They learn to groom the horses, and how to train them. That's the ranch's main focus."

Of course it was. She should have known that. "You're in the horse-training business, then," she concluded.

"No," Garrett corrected, "we're in the teen-training business."

"I don't understand." As far as she was concerned, he was bandying words around.

But then Garrett patiently spelled it all out for her.

"In order to train the horses, the ranch hands have to learn to discipline themselves. They have to have discipline before they can use it to train the horses. It's simple, really, once you see it in action. Works well for the ranch hands *and* the horses."

Kim supposed that it made sense—if it was actually true. But she could see how tempting it could be to use all this "free" labor, all these wayward men-children who supposedly were to be set straight.

Kim glanced around at the empty stalls. She assumed

that by the end of the day, they were all filled with horses. Horses that needed to be trained in order to yield a profit for the owners. Having actual ranch hands do the work that these boys were being made to do would prove to be almost prohibitively costly, she judged, so for Garrett and his brother, this was an ideal situation.

Still, there was a part of her—long buried—that wanted to believe what this drop-dead gorgeous cowboy was telling her. That they were doing all this for the boys. Garrett did appear proud and earnest when he'd gone over the cursory details of the way the ranch operated, but then, she'd come across a lot of earnest individuals who were anything *but*. To a person, they were out for themselves, everyone else be damned.

Were Garrett and his brother the same way?

Probably.

"Sounds like a nice world you have here," she told him, thinking that was what he was hoping to hear her say. If he lowered his guard, then maybe she could eventually get the truth out of him—whatever that was.

For now, she would make noises like a true believer and see where that got her.

"It actually is," Garrett agreed, then the corners of his mouth curved as he told her, "but you don't believe that."

"I didn't say that," she protested, doing her best to look upset and offended by his accusation.

The expression on Garrett's face told her that he wasn't buying into her protest. "You didn't have to. I can see it in your eyes."

Okay, so maybe he was more perceptive than she'd given him credit for. That just meant she would have to up her game—but before she did, she became aware of something.

"You don't exactly look upset."

"I'm not," he admitted. "It's only normal for you to be skeptical. That's what you do for a living, isn't it?" It was a rhetorical question on his part. "Examine the evidence before making a conclusion?"

She wished, Kim thought. But he had the wrong impression and she needed to set him straight before he got carried away.

"I'm not an investigative reporter," she told him before going on to explain the difference between that and what she did.

But Garrett interrupted her again before she had the chance to even get into the last part. What he said took her completely by surprise.

"Maybe you should be," Garrett told her with sincerity.

Stunned, she was thrown completely off guard for a moment by his simple suggestion. She'd spent so much time defending what she did, to her parents, to her sisters and, at times, to Stan when she tried to get him to give her something with teeth to write.

And now here was this sexy-looking cowboy telling her that he thought she had the stuff to write a more in-depth piece than what she was doing, to go beyond fluff to substance, something major she could be proud of.

It took the wind out of her sails and made her look at him in an entirely different light.

More than that, it made her shift from the mental stance she'd assumed to one that took a closer, more favorable look at his side—even if she didn't consciously realize it at first.

Chapter Six

Initially, she'd tried to talk Garrett out of coming along with her—although, if she was being strictly honest about it, he wasn't "coming along" with her. He was leading the way. And she had to admit, it wasn't as if she weren't directionally challenged.

After conducting an abbreviated tour of the stable and the bunkhouse, both of which, she noted, were conspicuously empty this time of the day, Garrett had commented that she was probably tired and might like to go to town in order to settle in at the hotel. That was when he'd offered to accompany her to Forever.

While the offer was secretly welcome, she did feel guilty about it.

"I've already taken up a lot of your time and I don't want to make it look like I'm taking advantage of you," she told him. "That'll give your brother something else to hold against me."

Garrett sighed as he shook his head. People from the big city tended to be a lot more guilt ridden than they were out here. Had to be something in the water, he decided.

"Jackson's not holding anything against you now. He just has a routine to adhere to and anything new kind of throws him for a little bit. It takes him a while to come around. Hell, he's still adjusting to married life," Garrett confided, "and he likes to tackle one thing at a time."

"Still—" she began to protest, really not wanting to get on Jackson's bad side. If anything, that would make writing the story more difficult—and she'd wind up having to stay longer, which she wouldn't welcome at all.

"I'll really feel terrible if you get lost," Garrett had gone on to say. "Going in with you won't take much out of my day and besides, Jackson's got it all covered," he'd told her, nodding back toward the corral.

She hadn't been all that sure, judging by the expression on the older brother's face, but given her annoying penchant for getting lost, she decided that agreeing to let Garrett lead the way into town wasn't a bad idea. While she believed in maintaining her independence, she wasn't a fanatic about it—especially if it got her lost.

"Well, if you put it that way," she'd said, surrendering, "I can't have you feeling bad, so I guess I'll take you up on your offer."

He'd seen right through her, but he'd grinned, anyway as he said, "Thank you." There was amusement dancing in those captivating blue eyes of his.

This time, rather than taking his horse, he'd taken a rather battered-looking truck for the proposed trip. And while Wicked was definitely more impressive looking than the cowboy's truck, she felt more at ease following the vehicle.

She could also drive faster because she wasn't afraid of hitting the truck the way she had been of colliding with the horse.

So it wasn't until Garrett had pulled up in front of

a five-story building that looked brand-new and she stopped behind him, quickly getting out, that she had a chance to really look around the area.

Leaving his truck where it was, Garrett walked over to her as she stood beside her rented sedan.

"Something wrong?" he asked.

She turned around to look at him. "This is Forever?" she asked, sounding a little uncertain, as if she didn't know if this was a town or a rest stop.

Garrett inclined his head in a quick nod. "For better or worse," he confirmed whimsically.

Her bemused expression turned quizzical. "Where's the rest of it?"

"Coming any day now," he answered, managing to keep the grin off his face for all of about ten seconds. And then he couldn't help himself. He laughed at the rather bewildered expression on her face. "Forever is a work in progress," he explained. "Progress isn't going too fast, though. For instance, this hotel wasn't here a year and a half ago."

So he had told her earlier. It still didn't make any sense to her. Kim took a deep breath, telling herself she was going to survive this and it would be behind her very, very soon.

"Out of sheer curiosity, what did people who came here do before the hotel was built?" she asked him.

"They stayed with friends."

"And if they didn't have any friends to stay with?" she prodded. Bunking in with friends wasn't always as easily accomplished as this cowboy seemed to indicate. Her parents, for instance, didn't exactly welcome overnight guests with open arms, even if they were visiting from half a continent away. More likely than not, they would recommend a local hotel to whoever wanted to visit for longer than a few hours. That obviously hadn't been an option here two years ago.

"Then they would just be passing through Forever on their way to somewhere else," he told her. "Nobody comes to Forever as part of some sort of a tourist package. There *are* no tourist attractions around here. This isn't Dallas or Houston," he pointed out. "It's a bunch of ranches with a diner and a saloon named Murphy's in the middle—and a general store for anyone who wants to cook their own meals instead of eating at the diner."

"What about the reservation?" she asked suddenly.

The question caught him by surprise. He wasn't accustomed to talking about the reservation. "What about it?" he asked warily.

She wondered if he realized that his face had clouded over ever so slightly—had she trod on his toes, touching a topic she wasn't supposed to? Or was he just naturally protective of a place people associated him with?

"Nothing," she answered innocently. "You just mentioned the ranches, but you didn't say anything about the reservation."

Garrett shrugged in a vague, dismissive manner. "Not all that much to say. The reservation's an enclosed world. Some people leave it, some stay their whole lives."

For a long time, it had been a tough place to live. It was only in recent years that things had begun to change and its inhabitants had started to thrive.

"So it's like Forever," Kim concluded.

He supposed she had a point. "The same, but different," he acknowledged. "Want me to walk you in?" Garrett asked, nodding at the hotel and effectively changing the subject.

"I've been walking on my own since I was eleven months old."

The amusement was back in his eyes. "Been checking into hotels for that long, have you?"

It took her a second, but his question made her see how she'd become *too* defensive. "Sorry, I didn't mean to sound ungrateful. I'm just not used to anyone offering their help like that."

He sincerely doubted that was true. Not the way she looked. Men probably fell all over themselves, trying to render her "assistance" she undoubtedly didn't need or want.

But he tempered his response, careful not to give offense. "I'm surprised. I'd have thought that you'd be on the receiving end of chivalry a lot."

"Chivalry?" she repeated.

"That's the modern code word for it, isn't it? Otherwise, a woman gets insulted because she thinks it means that a man doesn't think she's capable of getting things done."

"Things can get a little complicated," she acknowledged and then she added, "Thanks for everything," as she took her suitcases out of the trunk of the car.

He had no idea why he'd assumed that she didn't have luggage with her. He'd turned to leave but stopped and came around to the back of her car to take her suitcases. There were two, along with something he'd once heard referred to as a makeup case. In her place, he wouldn't have packed enough things to fit into the makeup case, much less two suitcases.

"I thought you said you weren't really going to stay here that long."

She still held on to the suitcases, not letting him take possession of them. "I never actually said," she pointed out.

"I read between the lines," he admitted. "But this looks like you're planning on staying in Forever for at least six months."

"Hardly," she told him. "This is just several days' worth of clothing."

"Looks more like you're smuggling a department store's spring lineup," he countered. Since she wasn't relinquishing the suitcases, he put his hand over hers on top of them. "I'll take these in for you."

Ever independent, Kim went on holding the suitcases. "No, I can—"

But somehow, he managed to take possession of the luggage and started walking into the hotel ahead of her.

Chivalry, she thought, shaking her head.

Lengthening her stride, Kim hustled to catch up. "You don't listen very well, do you?" she accused once she was walking beside him again.

Garrett laughed. Reaching the front desk, he placed the suitcases on the floor beside it. "My mother would say that's an improvement. She used to complain that I didn't listen at all," he told her.

Kim could empathize with his mother. "Poor woman, she must have had her hands filled with you."

There was no point in denying it. While Jackson was the one who gave his mother more than her share of grief, he wasn't exactly a slouch in that department, either. "She did."

"Where is she now?" Kim asked him. "I'd like to

talk to her." Actually, she wanted to meet the woman who raised Garrett. She had a feeling it would give her a lot of insight into the man he had become.

"So would I," Garrett admitted, growing just the slightest bit somber for a moment. "She died some years back."

She should have checked that out before she ever came here, Kim upbraided herself. Things like that were a matter of public record.

"Oh, I'm sorry."

"Yeah, me, too," he replied quietly.

"You don't know how lucky you are." When he raised an eyebrow, questioning her statement, Kim explained, "To feel that way about your mother."

"You don't feel that way about yours?" he said, coming to the only logical conclusion possible.

"She won't let me," she told him quietly. Quickly, she shook off the moment. That had been sharing too much and she needed him to leave.

As the receptionist, a woman who looked no older than about twenty and whose name tag read Miranda Perry, came up to the desk, Kim spared her guide one last glance.

"I'll take it from here. Thanks," she told him.

That was his cue to leave, Garrett thought.

Except that he wasn't in all that much of a hurry to go. So he hung back a couple more minutes on the pretext of verbally tying up loose ends.

"I'll be by tomorrow morning to take you back to the ranch," he told her. "Nine okay with you? I could come by earlier if you want."

"No need to come by at all," she assured him. "I'll find my own way."

"I'm sure you can," he said soothingly, as if trying to get through to a willful child, "I'll just feel better if I came for you."

She didn't want to argue over the point. If she changed her mind in the morning, she could always just take off on her own. It wasn't as if she lacked transportation.

"Okay, have it your way," she agreed, but added a stipulation. "Make it eight o'clock."

The revised schedule pleased him. "Even better. That'll give us time to have breakfast at Miss Joan's," he added.

"Miss Joan's?" she asked, waiting for more of an explanation.

"That's the way everyone refers to the diner. Miss Joan owns it and runs it," he told her.

This town was beginning to sound positively claustrophobic, Kim thought, mentally squirming inside. "Let me guess, that's the only place to eat in town."

"Other than eating at someone's house, yes," Garrett agreed.

Instead of commenting—or expressing her total disbelief, Kim turned to look at the young woman behind the counter.

"What about the hotel?" she asked. "Isn't there a restaurant on the premises?" All the hotels she was familiar with had not only one restaurant, but at least a couple, if not more, to choose from.

"Not yet," Miranda told her, but she looked exceedingly hopeful as she added, "but we're working on it. They might start building a coffee shop here by the middle of next year."

"Too long to wait for breakfast," Kim commented sarcastically. She thought of something else and looked at Garrett. "And that place you mentioned before... Murphy's, I think?"

"It's Murphy's," he agreed, then tactfully added, "They're technically not open at that hour in the morning."

She couldn't see a place turning its back on so many potential customers. That just didn't make sense, but then, she was beginning to think that was typical of this backward town.

"They just serve lunch and dinner?" she asked him.

"No," he corrected, "They just serve drinks." And then, because he wanted to be strictly correct, he added, "And pretzels and nuts, but that's not exactly good for you as a steady diet."

Kim stared at him. And then it dawned on her what was going on. Okay, she got it. This was all a joke. *No* place was this backward and strange.

"You're pulling my leg, aren't you?" she asked.

"Not that it's not a tempting thought," Garrett allowed, "But no, ma'am, I'm not."

"'Ma'am'?" Kim repeated incredulously. When had she crossed that line? "Really?"

"I could call you by your first name if you want," he offered.

That made it feel too personal, but better that than making her feel as if there was a squadron of Boy Scouts waiting to take her across the street—if this place *had* streets.

"Anything is better than 'ma'am,'" she told him. "That makes me feel like I'm stoop-shouldered with one foot in the grave."

His eyes slid over her slowly. As slowly as the smile spread out on his lips.

"You're certainly not that," he assured her.

Garrett was standing much too close, she thought, and while the idea of moving in even closer was not without its genuinely enticing merits, she didn't want to do that while there was an audience watching—and Miranda Perry hadn't even moved her eyes from them in the last few minutes.

It was as if the young woman thought she was watching her own personal enactment of some kind of very stilted romantic comedy.

With this in mind, Kim moved back.

Garrett took his cue from her. "I'll let you settle in and I'll be back in the morning—unless you'd like me to stick around," he suddenly suggested.

The offer didn't surprise her. He was making a move on her, Kim thought. She wasn't sure if she was more flattered than annoyed by that, or vice versa. In any case, she wanted to do a little exploring for herself first before she got back to being under the brothers' wings—or thumbs, whatever the case actually was.

Conducting interviews around town before she went back to the ranch might prove to be very useful.

"Tomorrow morning will be fine," she told Garrett, then added after a beat, "Bright and early."

"You got it," he promised. "Take good care of her, Miranda," he instructed, addressing the woman behind the reception desk. "See you tomorrow," he told Kim and then, with that, he took his leave.

Kim turned her attention to the receptionist, who was staring after Garrett a full minute after he had disappeared through the front entrance.

"You two know each other?" Kim asked her. Maybe she could start by interviewing her, she thought, then immediately changed her mind. This Miranda person looked as if she had a huge crush on Garrett. She could tell that she wasn't going to get anything useful out of her.

Miranda blinked, as if coming to.

Kim had no doubts that for a moment there, the receptionist had been lost in a fantasy world of her own making, population two.

"Sure," she answered with a huge grin. "Everyone knows everyone else here in Forever." Her smile dimmed a couple of watts, but was still exceedingly bright as she looked toward the entranceway again, as if hoping that Garrett had forgotten something and was going to double back any second. "Forever's cozy like that."

Her wistful tone wasn't lost on Kim. "I'll just bet it is," she murmured.

She saw Miranda flush, lowering her eyes for a moment. And then the receptionist got down to business. "Will you be staying at the hotel long?"

"God, I hope not," Kim answered, then realized she should have kept that to herself. "I'm just here until I get the story down," she added. That only brought more confusion to the young face. She might as well explain it, Kim thought. "I'm doing a story on the Healing Ranch for *Western Times Magazine*."

Miranda shook her head, then said apologetically, "I'm afraid I never heard of it."

Now why doesn't that surprise me, Kim thought cryptically. She kept a smile pasted on her lips, all the while thinking that it was shaping up to be a rough uphill battle.

Chapter Seven

The room was nicer than she would have expected to find in the first hotel of a town like Forever.

Kim laughed to herself as she put her suitcases down beside the bed. She supposed that she had adjusted her expectations accordingly after realizing just how small, how *quaint* for lack of a better word, how removed from the beaten path—or better yet, from civilization—this place really was.

So when the hotel room that she entered proved to be just as modern looking as anything she was accustomed to back home, she was rather surprised. Granted, the room couldn't compare to a thousand-dollar-a-night suite, but the fact that the room didn't make her think of a renovated barn was a definite plus.

In fact, the room was so pleasant that for a moment, she gave serious consideration to hiding out in it for the rest of her stay in this backward burg.

But given that the hotel had no room service, or any other sort of food service for that matter, unless she was willing to lie around, listening to her stomach rumbling hungrily for half the night, she would to have to venture out eventually. She doubted that the diner Garrett had mentioned to her—Jane's or Judy's or Joan's, that was it, Joan's, she thought triumphantly—she doubted that the place had takeout and delivery.

Well, if the diner couldn't come to her, she might as well go to the diner. And since she was venturing out, she might as well hit all the so-called "high" spots— what were there? three, four, she guessed—and do a little "investigative" digging.

The thought of the word *investigative* had her smiling to herself again.

Maybe that cowboy was more insightful than she'd given him credit for. Maybe she actually *could* become one of those writers—a journalist rather than someone who was handed light, fluffy pieces that amounted to fillers in between the important stories, the stories people bought the magazines and the newspapers to read.

Kim frowned at her reflection in the mirror above the double chest of drawers.

She was getting ahead of herself. There probably *wasn't* anything to dig into, no story, big or otherwise, beneath the surface. Just a couple of brothers trying to make a buck—and managing to do a good deed or two while they were at it. They were probably clean, which was good for them, but bad for her story. A little double-dealing would have given the article some color. It would have kept it from being a boring piece.

Which brought her back to the idea that this would be a quick assignment. It wasn't going to write itself with her just sitting here, staring at the walls. She needed to get out there.

Changing into something a bit more casual and comfortable, Kim went out to get a second impression of— and a closer look at—Forever.

It was a town where *everything* was within walking distance.

The first place she found herself wandering by was Murphy's, the bar that Garrett had mentioned. He'd also said that the establishment was a saloon, but as far as she was concerned, that was semantics.

Besides, it was a place where they served alcohol and she'd learned a long time ago that people were more likely to talk once their tongues were loosened a little. What better loosening agent than alcohol?

"Afternoon, pretty lady," the tall, handsome man behind the counter said to her, accompanying his greeting with a quick smile and a quicker question. "My name is Brett. What's your pleasure? Something with an umbrella in it, or would you rather have a shot of something straight up?" Brett Murphy, the oldest of the three brothers who owned and ran Murphy's, asked.

"I'd like a shot of straight information, Brett," Kim told him, borrowing some of the words he'd used before adding, "And it's too early to drink."

Brett inclined his head. "For some, I'm sure. Others," he went on, nodding toward the heavyset man at the end of the bar nursing a glass with only a trace of an amber-colored liquid left in it, "have been here and at it for a while."

Kim glanced at her watch. "Really? This early?" she asked.

She was well aware that people didn't always adhere to a timetable when it came to drinking, but the ones who craved alcohol usually did so in private until an acceptable hour arrived. Obviously, that thought hadn't occurred to the man at the end of the bar.

"Ah, but it's always five o'clock somewhere," Brett

told her. "He's a regular, and believe it or not, he knows how to hold it. Poor devil would rather drown his liver than afflict his ears, listening to his wife enumerate all the ways he's disappointed her, starting with today and going back over the years."

"Colorful," she commented.

Brett's smile was good-natured. "That's one take on it." He continued polishing the counter in front of him just a little longer. "So, if I can't serve you something in a glass, what can I serve you?"

This was certainly going to be a simple matter, she thought. "What can you tell me about Garrett and Jackson White Eagle?"

Brett's mouth curved. "You're the writer," he said with a nod. "Kimberly Lee, right?" He made it sound like a question, extending his hand to her. "Nice to meet you," he said.

Kim blinked. "How do you know who I am?" she asked in surprise.

"It's a small town, darlin'. Not much happens here, so anything out of the ordinary gets around. Fast." Realizing that the dish towel was still in his hand, he placed it underneath the counter and settled in for a conversation. "What can I tell you about Garrett and Jackson?"

"First of all, are they natives?" Kim asked. When she saw the way the bartender's smile widened, she realized her mistake. She hadn't meant for it to sound as if she was asking about their heritage. "I mean to the area."

"Yes, born and bred," he answered. "They shared the same father, not the same mother." He couldn't number the brothers among his friends—they were usually too busy to come in and just socialize for a couple of hours—but he found them friendly enough when their paths *did* cross. "Had a rough time of it from what I hear. All I can say is that those boys turned out a lot better than some of the locals thought they would."

She'd taken her small notebook out and was making notes to herself. Using pad and pencil was rather old-fashioned, but it made her feel as if she had control over things.

"What about the Healing Ranch?" she asked.

Brett cocked his head, as if that could help him make sense of her question better. It didn't.

"What about it?"

"Well, they keep delinquents there. Has there been any trouble locally because of that?" She couldn't see how there hadn't been. The ranch wasn't exactly filled with choir boys and if those teens were being restricted on the ranch, that was definitely a recipe that guaranteed an explosion.

The only variable was time.

"Well, now, they don't really 'keep' delinquents," Brett pointed out, gently correcting her wrong impression. "That makes those boys they're working with sound like pets in a cage. That's not what they're all about. Jackson and Garrett take in troubled kids and turn them around, make them feel like they've got something to contribute."

She focused on the word *troubled*. That was just another way of saying delinquent.

"And nobody has a problem with that?" she asked. When he looked at her quizzically, she explained what she meant. "That they're housing teenagers who are on their way to becoming hardened criminals?"

Nobody he knew of was having a problem with the

boys the brothers were taking in. If anything, the town was rather proud of what they were accomplishing.

"It's the end result that matters, don't you think?" he asked her.

Kim didn't answer him. Instead, she continued to press her point.

"And you're okay with that? Having potential thieves and who knows what else living just on the outskirts of town, close enough to where you live to hear you breathe? Doesn't it ever worry you what might happen to the town if these kids ever got it into their collective heads to break out and take their frustrations out on the town?"

But Brett appeared entirely unfazed by what she was proposing. Leaning forward across the counter, he confided to her, "I wasn't a saint as a kid myself, so I get what Jackson and Garrett are doing. Good for them," he added with genuine feeling. "I'm not counting," he went on to add, "but I know they fixed a lot of kids in the last four years."

Kim put the notebook away in her purse and then slid off the stool.

"Thank you," she said primly, her tone calling an end to the interview.

It was obvious to Brett that he hadn't really convinced her of the brothers' selfless reasons for running the ranch. And he hadn't supplied the woman with what she was seeking—whatever that actually turned out to be.

"You're not going to find it, you know," he called after her as she began to leave.

Kim turned around to look at him, confused. "Find what?"

He'd taken out the dish towel again and was polishing his way down the counter, to the lone, exceptionally steady customer at the end of the bar. "Someone who has something bad to say about them. I mean, other than an out-and-out lie, you're not going to find any deep, dark secrets to play up about Jackson or Garrett or their ranch."

Kim gave the saloon owner the benefit of the doubt. "Maybe you're right," she said as she walked out.

The door creaked as it began to close behind her in slow motion.

"No maybe about it," Brett said under his breath. "But we've all gotta find our own truths," he added as he watched the woman walk past the window that looked out onto the sidewalk.

From the direction she'd taken, his guess was that she was headed for the general store next.

It was the same everywhere, Kim discovered to both her disappointment and considerable surprise.

If this had been an urban area rather than a tiny button of a rural town tucked away as an afterthought, she would have come across as many damaging words as she would have glowing ones. In the big city, people had more opinions, different takes on the same set of circumstances, she concluded.

Here everyone had nothing but praise for the two brothers.

"Especially Jackson," Jake Winterset, the man who ran the general store, told her. "I can remember, back in the day, thinking he was just going to burn himself out, running around with that no-good crowd of thugs he was hanging out with."

Her ears definitely perked up. "You mean there're

people here who aren't all sugar and spice?" she asked, struggling not to sound sarcastic. The bartender at Murphy's had led her to believe that this was all one big, harmonious family.

Maybe after a couple of drinks or so they were.

Jake laughed. "You bet there are. There was a time— not all that long ago—when people around here thought that Jackson would just be another casualty, another statistic to add to the pile of lives that had gone wrong. But Garrett's mother wasn't going to let Jackson do that to himself, even if he wasn't her flesh and blood.

"That little lady got her brother-in-law to take Jackson in hand. He turned Jackson around, made him into the man he is now. Jackson just took the lesson he learned and applied it to kids just like him. That became his mission in life."

Another glowing testimony.

Kim nodded, then thanked the store owner as she closed her notebook and started to tuck it away into her purse.

She was getting nowhere.

"What's the matter, can't find anyone to say anything bad about us?"

Her heart lunged into her throat as Kim swung around, away from the checkout counter, and all but crashed smack into Garrett who was standing right behind her.

Her pulse pounded wickedly. She told herself it was just because the big idiot had scared her. "What are you doing here?" she cried, startled.

Her voice was breathless and there was something extremely sexy about that, Garrett thought. For a moment, with his hands on her shoulders to help steady her on her feet, he felt himself getting lost in her eyes.

He pulled back.

"I didn't mean to scare you," he told her, releasing Kim after a beat. "I just thought I might take you to an early dinner, seeing as how this is going to be your first night here."

"You don't have to take me anywhere," she informed him. "I can pay for my own dinner."

He would have to readjust his thinking around this one, Garrett counseled himself. He hadn't meant to make her think he was talking down to her.

"Then I can just sit across from you and eat my own dinner," he said, effortlessly switching gears. Nodding goodbye to Jake, Garrett opened the front door and held it for her, his implication clear.

After a long moment, Kim shrugged carelessly and crossed the threshold, going outside.

"Doing a little research?" he asked her amicably as he followed her out.

Okay, that was just too spot-on to be a casual guess on his part. Did he and his brother have spies in town? People who owed them favors, or better yet, were under their thumb and too afraid to just break away? "Did they call you?"

He gazed at her, confusion marking his handsome face. "Did who call me?"

"Playing dumb doesn't become you," she informed him. But when he didn't say anything, she added, "The people I talked to about your work, did they call you?"

His expression was the picture of innocence—which was why she didn't believe him when he said, "No."

"Then how would you know I was doing research?" she challenged.

"Simple," he answered. "Because that's what it looked like when I walked in on you." He stopped walking for a moment, wanting to make something perfectly clear to her. "Look, Jackson and I have got nothing to hide. You want to know something, you just ask either one of us, we'll tell you. The *truth*," he emphasized in case she was having any doubts about that.

She found herself wanting to believe him—and thinking herself dumb for the same reason. "So there are no kickbacks involved?" she asked bluntly.

She wanted everything clear, so he was going to lay it all out for her. "Other than literally from some of the guys when they first get here, no, no kickbacks of any kind," he answered firmly, then asked, "Anything else?"

He was so ready to talk, it threw her. She was certain that he was just playing her, but she would need to arm herself and come out firing, so for now, she had no questions.

But she would, she promised herself. And very, very soon.

"Yes."

Garrett braced himself, not really sure what to expect. "Shoot."

"Is there *really* only one place to eat in this town?" she asked.

Garrett laughed at the question. "Lots of places to eat in Forever," he told her. "But you have to be invited over to the people's house first."

She shook her head. The thought of just one restaurant in a town—even a small town—was completely

inconceivable to her, not to mention close to being un-
civilized.

"Why doesn't someone else open up a restaurant?"
she asked. "You, for instance."

His laugh was hearty, like a big burst of sunshine
that could be felt all over her body. "You stay in Forever
long enough, I'll let you sample some of my cooking.
That'll answer your question straight away."

"Okay, not you," she allowed. Not everyone could
cook, she knew that by her own limited skills. But there
had to be others in this place who had more of an enterprising take on things. If they couldn't cook, maybe
they could finance a small eatery and bring in someone
who could handle the food preparation. "But not everyone here can be culinary-challenged," Kim assumed.

"No, but the two best cooks in the whole town work
for Miss Joan. Why go through the mess of cooking
when all you have to do is head to Miss Joan's and get
yourself a meal that'll make your insides smile."

"Oh, come on, it can't be *that* good," she told Garrett skeptically.

To her surprise, he took her hand and pulled her
down the street.

"You're on," he told her. "We'll go over to Miss
Joan's and you tell me how you feel after you've eaten.
We'll make a friendly bet as to who's right."

"What do I get if I win?" she asked.

"The satisfaction of proving me wrong."

She shook her head. "Tempting, but I want more at
stake. How about, if I win, you tell me some deep, dark
secret about the school, you or your brother?"

"And if I win—which I will—what do I win?" he
asked.

"The satisfaction of being right." she told him, echoing the same words he had initially said to her.

And he returned the favor. "Good, but not good enough."

"If you win, I'll stop trying to find something damning to pin on your and your brother."

The expression on his face wasn't a humoring one. Rather, it was the kind of expression a parent wore when they realized that their child had to make their own mistakes in order to come to the same inevitable conclusion that was already being tendered to them—and rejected.

"Not much of a bet," he told her. "One way or another, you won't find anything. But okay, you're on." With that, he tugged on her hand again.

This time, she allowed him to lead her to their final destination—Miss Joan's.

Chapter Eight

The tall, thin older woman moving authoritatively and effortlessly behind the long lunch counter appeared to take no notice of the newest customers who had just walked into her diner. But anyone familiar with Miss Joan knew that she was very much aware that the number of customers in the diner had increased by two.

Garrett White Eagle had come in, bringing with him a woman who was the newest stranger to have arrived in Forever.

It wasn't so much that the diner owner possessed legendary eyes in the back of her head—although some of Forever's youngest residents would have been willing to swear that she did. She just had almost a sixth sense when it came to people.

A sense that had developed and evolved over the years, thanks to not only her interactions with her customers—and at one point or other, all of the residents of Forever passed through the door of her diner—but with people in general.

Miss Joan and her diner had been a part of Forever for as long as most of the people who lived in the town and outlying areas could remember. But Garland Chapin, who at 97 was officially Forever's oldest resident, remembered that the sharp-witted, hazel-eyed redhead had come into Forever from somewhere else a long, long time ago.

Just when, however, was another story.

When asked for specifics as to when she'd arrived and just where it was that she had come from, Garland's answer would always be the same.

"A gentleman never talks about a lady's past, or her age. That's between her and her maker." Which was why, whenever Garland's great-grandson brought the old man into the diner—occasions that were becoming fewer and farther in between—Miss Joan always made sure that anything Garland ordered was always on the house. As was his great-grandson's meal.

In a town of individuals, Miss Joan was as individual as they came. Married for a second time late in life—she never spoke of her first marriage and people knew better than to try to venture past the sadness in her eyes—she found happiness in being Harry Monroe's better half. But the only change in her life was the wedding ring on her hand.

As sharp-tongued as she was sharp-witted, Miss Joan dispensed unsolicited advice and reaped fierce loyalty in exchange. No one who came in contact with the feisty, opinionated woman remained indifferent to her for long. It was impossible.

"So this is it," Kim said, scanning the diner. It looked unremarkable to her, like any other diner. She saw no reason why some enterprising individuals hadn't decided to pull together their resources and open up another more appealing restaurant. It couldn't be all that hard.

When she moved closer to the front of the diner Kim

realized she was the unwitting subject of close scrutiny. Not just by the woman who owned the place but by everyone else in the diner. The din, not particularly loud when Garrett had opened the door, faded completely now.

All eyes, it seemed, had turned in their direction.

In *her* direction.

"You weren't kidding about there not being any kind of diversion in this town," she murmured to Garrett under her breath.

"That's enough, people. You're making the lady uncomfortable," Miss Joan announced in a voice that sounded as if it was equal parts gravel and whiskey. "You've all seen strangers before," the older woman added as a closing argument before turning her attention to Garrett and the woman he'd brought in. "There's a table right here," she said, indicating a small table for two directly to her right. As they each took a seat, Miss Joan crossed to the table. "Been wondering when you'd get around to coming here."

Kim assumed the woman was addressing Garrett but quickly realized that the owner of the diner was looking right at her. She hadn't even been in town for twenty-four hours. The woman couldn't have been *expecting* her. Could she?

"Excuse me?"

But Miss Joan waved away her own words, as well as the stranger's question. "Doesn't matter, you're here now." She focused her attention on Garrett's companion. "So, what'll it be? A cup of coffee to warm your hands, or a meal to warm your insides? Angel's specialty today is individual-sized quiche lorraine pies."

"Angel?" Kim repeated, glancing at the cowboy across from her for some insight.

Was that the woman's way of saying that the meal she was talking about tasted heavenly? For her part, Kim had to admit that she wouldn't have thought a meal like quiche lorraine would have found its way to a town that was fairly close to the border. It seemed that some sort of meal with a colorful Mexican or Spanish reference in its name would have been more in keeping with the town's location.

"Angel Rodriguez," Garrett said.

"My head cook," Miss Joan said proudly so that there would be no misunderstanding as to the woman's identity. "She just showed up in town one day and just started making magic happen in the kitchen." A deep, theatrical cough suddenly emerged behind Miss Joan from the area where the kitchen was contained. Miss Joan frowned, but she didn't look surprised. "Keep coughing like that, Eduardo, and you're going to choke to death. You were never in Angel's league and we both know it. I just kept you around after Angel started working here out of the goodness of my heart."

"You would have to have a heart to have some goodness in it, old woman," Eduardo informed her, raising his voice to be heard.

Miss Joan rolled her eyes. Not bothering to turn around toward the source of the voice, she merely waved a hand dismissively in its general direction. She and the silver-haired Eduardo went way back. He'd been working for her since before he'd had a single gray hair.

"Don't pay any attention to Eduardo," she told Kim. "He thought of himself as cock of the walk until Angel came around. Can't come to terms with the fact that she's so much better than he is at the same thing. But he has his moments," she concluded.

Looking from Garrett to the woman he'd brought in, Miss Joan asked, "So, what'll it be? Coffee? Or quiche? We've got other things," she said, tapping the menu she was holding against her. "But I think the quiche'll suit you just fine."

Kim hadn't eaten since before she'd gotten lost and right now, the thought of even biting into shoe leather was not completely abhorrent to her. Otherwise, she might have taken exception to having a choice made for her. But at the moment, she didn't care who chose the meal as long as it arrived quickly.

"Quiche it is, then," Kim replied.

"Good choice," Miss Joan proclaimed. "You, too, handsome?" she went on to ask, directing her attention to Garrett.

"I'll have whatever you recommend, Miss Joan," Garrett told her, adding "You know best" for good measure.

Miss Joan smiled, something that her patrons knew didn't happen all that often despite all her concern regarding the people of the town. "You might try passing that bit of wisdom along to your brother. I don't think he's willing to concede that yet."

Garrett winked at the woman, then assured her with a knowing smile, "He knows, Miss Joan. He's just too stubborn to admit it."

"Just like his uncle that way," Miss Joan agreed with a sharp nod of her head. "Be right back with your orders. In the meantime, have some coffee. On the house," she told Kim, taking her cup and placing it right side up, then filling it.

Garrett turned his own cup right side up. "Me, too?" he quipped, knowing better.

"You pay like everyone else, smart guy," she informed Garrett. "First cup of coffee to a newcomer's always on the house," she explained to Kim in what was almost an aside—except that everyone in the diner was familiar with her rule.

"You have another uncle?" Kim asked Garrett, waiting a moment until after the other woman had gone to post their orders in the kitchen.

"No, just Sam," Garrett told her, then explained Miss Joan's reference regarding his uncle's stubbornness. "He and Miss Joan had something going on for a while years ago."

Backstories always aroused her interest. "What happened?"

He shrugged. "Whatever was going on stopped. Neither one of them would talk about it—" not that he hadn't tried to find out "—and they were always polite to one another. Personally, I always felt that Sam thought he couldn't ask a woman to share his life with him because he didn't think he had all that much to share."

He looked genuinely sad as he told her, "My uncle was a very proud man. Miss Joan had her pride, too, so she wasn't about to try to make him change his mind and he wasn't about to offer her a life where he couldn't provide her with at least the same sort of lifestyle she was accustomed to."

"They could have shared," Kim pointed out. "It shouldn't have mattered if she had more and he had less. It would've added up to the same total as if he had more and she had less."

But Garrett shook his head. "Not the Navajo way. And at least Miss Joan found someone. She got married a few years ago. Her husband lets her have her way, so they get along just fine. I guess you could say that things turned out all right for Miss Joan."

She had to ask. "And your uncle?"

Sam had been married once, but he'd lost his wife in childbirth and the baby soon after that. Garrett felt that was something his uncle wouldn't have wanted outsiders to know about, so he kept the story to himself.

Instead, he told Kim, "The most important thing to my uncle was family honor—and he turned Jackson around, made him into a decent human being, so I guess he felt fulfilled."

She'd already gotten the image of Jackson being the bad boy of the family—which left her wondering about Garrett.

"How about you?" she asked him. "Did you make your uncle feel 'fulfilled?'"

Garrett laughed softly to himself.

"Sam never had to 'turn' me around from anything so I guess I didn't really 'fulfill' him," he told her with a good-natured shrug. "I was just there."

She wasn't sure if she bought into that, at least not entirely. "You never wanted to be like your big brother, do the kind of daring things he was doing and getting away with?"

"Oh, sure, I wanted to," he admitted. There was a kind of thrilling allure to what Jackson was doing back then, at least to the naive kid he had been at the time. "But I didn't have a tough skin like he did. He got away with things, and when he didn't, when he got caught— and this is the part that really scared my mother—he would just tough it out, put up with the punishment and act like it was no big deal. Me, I wasn't resilient like that. I guess you might say that I was too scared to be bad."

She wasn't sure just what goaded her on, but she found that she couldn't stand by and let him just shrug off what he'd done. In her eyes, it took a lot of courage not to give in to temptation.

"Maybe you just had too much integrity to be bad," she pointed out.

His eyes met hers. "That's a much nicer way to say it," he agreed.

There was that grin of his again, Kim thought, barely able to keep from squirming. That grin that made her bones feel as if they were made of paraffin and getting much too close to the heat for anyone's own good.

With effort, she focused on the conversation and not on the way he watched her.

"It's all in the way you say something," she told him, adding, "I make my living with words. I'd be a pretty poor writer if I didn't know how to reword something and make it sound good."

Miss Joan picked that moment to materialize from behind the counter with their order. Kim had to struggle not to sigh out loud with relief.

"There you go," Miss Joan announced, sliding small golden-crusted pie dishes, one at a time, in front of each of them. "Angel's quiche lorraine, otherwise known as bits of heaven. Let me know if you need anything else," she told them as she began to withdraw.

"I'd like to talk with you later on today, or tonight, whenever you have a moment," Kim told the diner owner.

Miss Joan turned back to look at her. For the moment, she remained just where she'd stopped. "About Jackson, or the ranch?" she asked.

It took effort to keep from looking at the woman in complete surprise. No one else she'd approached so far today had managed to guess why she'd sought them out. That Miss Joan had—and so easily—impressed her. She supposed this went right along with the woman's so-called all-knowing legend.

"Both," Kim answered.

Miss Joan's eyes shifted toward Garrett and then she nodded in his direction. "About him, too?"

Kim avoided looking at the man across from her. She hadn't wanted to say that with Garrett sitting right there, but now that Miss Joan had taken the initiative, she couldn't very well lie about it. So instead she said, "He's part of it."

Miss Joan nodded, taking it all in. "I'll find some time," the woman promised her before moving on to another patron.

Garrett couldn't see the point of talking to the woman if all Kim was after was some sort of juicy gossip. Miss Joan wasn't the type to pass on half truths and baseless speculations. "You do realize that Miss Joan's kind of partial to Jackson—and to me—because of my uncle."

"Still might be kind of interesting to hear what the woman has to say. I'm pretty good at reading between the lines."

He studied her for a moment. "What if that's all there is are the lines?" he asked. "No insight, no meaningful breakthroughs, just a bunch of busy lines, running into each other?"

She wasn't in the mood for philosophical conversations—and was frankly surprised that Garrett would have opted for one. He definitely didn't seem like the type. But it was beginning to dawn on her that not everything or everyone in and around Forever was 100 percent predictable—or exactly what they seemed.

"Let me worry about that," she told Garrett.

Her mind on the situation, Kim really wasn't paying attention to the food that was in front of her. For the most part, although she enjoyed the occasional pricey restaurant with its appetizing, rather undersized servings, she didn't really pay all that much attention to what she was eating.

Instead, she was accustomed to bringing her fork to her mouth and consuming whatever was at the end of that fork. Very infrequently did something she was eating actually register with her. It usually happened when the taste proved to be too tart or too bitter. Occasionally, the same end result occurred if something tasted too sweet.

The word *delicious* didn't figure into her radar scale.

But when the first forkful of quiche passed her lips and the flavor immediately registered with her tongue, her eyes widened in utter surprise as if she was a five-year-old at her own surprise birthday party.

"I see Angel has worked her magic yet again." Garrett instantly noticed the change in her expression. He found her expression both endearing and arousing. Neither had a place in his day-to-day life.

"This is *good*," she cried the same way she might have announced that the puddle she thought she was crossing was actually a pool of liquid gold. "*Really* good."

Garrett's grin widened. He was enjoying just watching her. Her reaction was completely unabashed. "Miss Joan warned you."

"No, I mean *really, really* good. This woman, this master chef Miss Joan has in her kitchen, is wasting her time here," Kim told him, still amazed at the explosion of savory flavors dancing around in her mouth.

"She's cooking for people she likes, working for a woman she looks at as a second mother and is earning quite a decent living for this area. How is this wasting her time?" he asked.

"She could be earning a fortune, running her own place, putting out a line of cooking products, maybe have her own cooking show on a cable network."

There was no end to the ways this Angel who was currently working in Miss Joan's kitchen could capitalize on her talent, Kim thought. With the right sort of exposure and maybe a little bit of a helping hand from—

"I don't think any of what you just mentioned actually interests Angel," Garrett told her, shooting down the rest of her innovative plans, and making them crash and burn. "Angel came here from somewhere else. She settled here—and *stayed* here—because she wanted to. She married the guy who rescued her from her abusive boyfriend who came to Forever looking for her." Didn't she get it? Garrett wondered. "Angel's life here is what makes her happy," he emphasized for Kim's benefit. "I don't think all those things you enumerated would do the same for her. It's like Miss Joan says—everyone's got to find their own form of 'happy.' I think it's safe to say that Angel found hers."

Then I guess this Angel is one up on me, Kim thought.

Chapter Nine

"How far away is the reservation from here?" Kim asked.

The question had just come out of the blue without any preamble or warning, catching Garrett completely off guard.

They were still sitting in the diner, eating. The place itself had only grown more crowded as people came in to grab a late supper. The din had increased, as well, but there was no missing what Kim had asked.

"Why? Do you want to have a tour of the reservation?"

It was the first thing that had occurred to him. Most people who casually requested a tour thought that all reservations looked like the quaint villages that had once been stereotypically depicted in old-fashioned Westerns, or, at the very least, were places of interest to tour. They had no idea what an actual reservation looked like. The one near Forever, where he had lived on with his mother until he was five, had once been the very picture of abject poverty. He and his mother had moved from there into Ben White Eagle's house, which wasn't all that much better, but it was still better than where he'd lived before.

Because of a few good people working together, both from within the reservation and from Forever, the homes on the reservation could now all boast that they had heat in the winter and running water all year round.

The reservation itself, as well as the houses, which were works in progress, were all coming along, much the way the Healing Ranch was coming along.

Slowly, but surely.

"Well, I wasn't thinking of a tour, actually," Kim confessed.

His curiosity now aroused, Garrett asked, "What were you thinking of, 'actually'?"

"Are you and your brother, I don't know, members?" Kim asked, searching for the word she needed to describe what she was attempting to say.

"Members?" Garrett repeated. When she nodded her head in response, he still wasn't sure what she was getting at. "Are you asking me if we're Navajos?"

She shook her head, frustrated. "No, what I'm trying to find out is did you ever live on the reservation? Are you and Jackson considered part of that community?"

Garrett knew that he was far more open about his life than Jackson was, but then, in Jackson's defense, he hadn't been knocked around nearly as much as his older brother had been. But despite his openness, even *he* was leery of a certain line of questioning and he had no idea what this woman with the incredible eyes was ultimately getting at. But so far, it didn't make him feel comfortable.

"Where's this going, Kim?" he finally asked. He wasn't about to answer her question until she answered his.

Pressing her lips together, Kim tried again. For a

skillful writer, there were times, such as now, when her words seemed to be failing her. "I just thought that if you and your brother were actually part of the reservation, the two of you shouldn't have too much trouble getting a casino going there."

The corners of Garrett's mouth curved in an ironic smile. She had no idea how Jackson felt about gambling. One of the reasons that their father never had any money to pay for basic things like food and shelter was because whatever money Ben White Eagle hadn't drank away, he'd gambled away. Consequently, Jackson stoically steered clear of both. That meant that running a casino would be the very *last* thing that Jackson would want to do. She didn't understand that the reservation wanted to preserve its culture, not necessarily cash in on a casino.

"And why would we want to do that?" Garrett asked her.

"I just thought that it might be an alternate way to make money. A large amount of money," she emphasized. "From the little that I know, it seems easier for a casino to be operated on reservation land than it does to even *try* to open one outside of it."

Garrett shook his head. "Jackson wouldn't want any part of that—"

"And you?" she asked pointedly.

"I want whatever Jackson wants," he answered simply. "This is a family venture—and what'll it take to convince you that this isn't about the money for us?" He could feel himself losing his patience with this line of questions she kept returning to—and that sort of thing didn't happen very often. He was the easygoing one.

"Don't get me wrong, I've got nothing against money

and I like the idea of having a little extra put by in case we run aground during tougher times—but strictly for the money is *not* how Jackson operates. He's running the ranch in order to do the most amount of good, not to try to amass some kind of nice retirement fund for himself and for me."

Maybe it was time to just cut bait here and admit he was wrong. At least Jackson would get a kick out of it.

With that in mind, Garrett said, "Look. I talked my brother into agreeing to have you come to the ranch and poke around, ask questions. But if you keep insisting on looking for angles that aren't there, then maybe he was right and this really *was* a bad idea." He wanted to give her a graceful way out, so he said, "I can call your editor and tell him we've changed our minds. No reflection on you," he added. "I'll pay for your dinner and when you finish, you're free to leave."

Garrett started to get up from their table, but Kim caught him by the wrist to stop him. On his feet, he looked at her, waiting.

"I'm sorry," Kim quickly apologized, although the words didn't come to her tongue easily. Her entire childhood had seemed like one huge apology to her at the time. Her parents always managed to twist things so that she was forever apologizing for doing things—or not doing things. "I really didn't mean to insult you and your brother."

Garrett remained where he was—but he didn't sit down yet. "You didn't knowingly insult us." He got that part. "But there's no point in continuing this if I can't convince you that the Healing Ranch is much more important to Jackson—and to me—than dollar signs on an Excel spread sheet."

"I'm convinced," she told him even though it wasn't 100 percent true. But for Garrett to be willing to turn his back on an article about the ranch published in a national magazine told her he felt very strongly about what he was telling her. "Let's start over," she suggested.

"Not over," Garrett corrected, sitting down at the table again. "We can pick up where we left off." He looked into her eyes. "Just as long as we understand each other."

"Okay," she agreed. "Just as long as *you* understand that I'm accustomed to there always being some kind of angle behind everything. Where I come from, altruism is a word in a dictionary, not a fact of daily life—or even occasional life," she amended. And then she smiled at him, thinking that maybe it was all right to do a feel-good story once in a while—as long as the details were accurate. "You and your brother and this ranch for wayward boys takes some getting used to."

Garrett thought that she was saying that it would take her longer to write the article than she'd initially anticipated. "You're welcome to stay to write it as long as you like."

She laughed shortly. "Easy for you to say, but I think my editor's only willing to pay for a three-day stay at the hotel." Which meant that no matter what kind of a story she found—good or bad—she only had three days in which to write it.

"You could stay at the ranch," he suggested. He'd assumed she'd be here for longer than that. Garrett felt a twinge of disappointment and did what he could to dismiss it.

Kim shook her head. "I'm sure your brother would love that."

Garrett didn't argue the point one way or the other. He knew that Jackson wouldn't be thrilled about her staying with them, but the ranch house, like the ranch itself, was half his and that gave him the right to extend an invitation to whomsoever he chose—and he chose her.

"We've got the room," he told her, focusing on the positive aspect.

Because Garrett's offer intrigued her, she proposed a compromise. "Let me see how much I can get done in the next couple of days. Maybe Stan'll let me extend my stay if he likes what I've written and pick up a few extra days at the hotel."

"Fair enough."

Looking down, he noticed that despite the topic and the momentary possibility that their association was terminating, the woman had still managed to polish off her meal.

"Ready for dessert?" he asked.

She laughed at the question. "I was born ready for dessert, but I think I should finish this quiche first." In response to her words, his grin widened. It was having a definite effect on her stomach, she thought, feeling her stomach muscles tighten. Still, she couldn't get herself to look away. "What?"

Garrett nodded toward the empty pie dish. "You finished it."

"No, I didn't," she protested, then looked down at the dish. "Yes, I did," she amended, stunned. "How did that happen?"

His grin deepened—as did her reaction. "One forkful at a time is my guess."

She felt a flush of color creeping up her cheeks. Embarrassed, she could only laugh at herself. "I guess my attention was elsewhere."

"I guess so," he agreed, doing his best to appear moderately serious. He failed. "So, about that dessert—"

Seeing as how, in a roundabout fashion, he had gotten her to sample the best quiche lorraine she'd ever had grace her tongue, Kim saw no reason to ask to see a menu.

"I'll just have whatever you want to have," she told Garrett.

What I want to have isn't on the menu.

The thought flashed through Garrett's mind, catching him by surprise and as off guard as her question about the reservation had.

Except that this time around, the "surprise" he felt had been accompanied by a wave of intense warmth that he experienced from the roots of his hair down to the bottom of his toes. The sensation took a great deal of effort to banish from his system.

Ignoring it was utterly impossible.

Finally, because she was watching him and he really didn't want the moment to become awkward—after all, he had just won her over to his side—he forced his attention back to the actual subject under discussion. Dessert.

"How does apple pie à la mode sound to you?" Garrett asked her—finding he had to struggle to make his mind stay on point.

"Absolutely terrific," she confessed, flashing an appreciative grin that told him all he needed to know about Kim and her ongoing relationship with vanilla ice cream.

Absolutely terrific, his brain echoed, but unlike Kim,

he wasn't thinking about apple pie or the vanilla ice cream on top of it. He was thinking about something a lot closer to him at the moment than either of the two items.

AFTER THE DESSERT had come and gone, Kim allowed herself a second to sigh contentedly, then thanked Garrett for his company as she began to excuse herself from the table.

Apparently, he'd assumed that they were leaving together. "Are you going somewhere?" he asked her.

She nodded in response. "I told Miss Joan I wanted to talk to her," she reminded him of what she'd initially said to the woman after he'd introduced them. "And I thought, in the interest of time, I'd get it over with now if she has a moment."

He wouldn't advise it, but Garrett knew better than to attempt to tell her—or any female he knew—what to do. "Unless you really mean that—or can talk really, really fast—you're going to find that she's probably too busy to spare any time."

Since he seemed to know so much about the woman, she asked him, "When isn't she busy?"

Garrett didn't even stop to think. "When she's asleep would be my guess—but probably even then," he reconsidered. In all the years he'd known her, the woman never seemed to stop to rest. She just kept going like the force of nature everyone knew she was.

But Kim wasn't about to be dissuaded. "I'll give now a try," she decided. Rising from the table, she added, "I'll see you tomorrow."

Garrett got up, as well, watching as the woman who had more than piqued his interest made her way to the counter. He discovered that he liked watching her walk. Specifically, he liked watching the rhythm of her hips when she walked.

To the surprise of several of the waitresses, Kim went around the counter and walked right behind it.

Since she didn't see Miss Joan anywhere, she assumed that the woman was in the kitchen. Without hesitation, Kim went right through the swinging double doors that were on the left behind the counter.

She wound up all but colliding with Miss Joan who was on her way out of the kitchen.

Startled, Miss Joan and Kim simultaneously took a step back from one another.

"Is now a bad time?" Kim asked, trying not to sound as breathless as the just-barely-avoided collision had made her.

"It depends on for what," Miss Joan qualified. "Is this a bad time to ask for seconds on dessert? No. A bad time to ask for anything else? Definitely yes."

But even as Miss Joan started to walk away from her, Kim still didn't give up. "I thought that maybe I could ask you to tell me about Jackson and Garrett White Eagle."

Miss Joan turned around and looked at her. "Tell you what?"

Kim shrugged in response, not to indicate indifference, but to indicate that the field was wide-open on that. "Anything."

Miss Joan blew out a breath, as if she thought that the question she was being asked was frivolous, as well as useless and that she was being needlessly bothered to talk about something that was already a given.

Acting as if every moment was precious and she

had few to spare for an outsider who asked rhetorical questions, Miss Joan told her, "Jackson and Garrett are good, decent boys who work hard and wound up making something of themselves despite the poor hands that they were initially dealt."

"You mean being born on the reservation," Kim assumed.

Miss Joan's pencil-thin eyebrows narrowed into almost an accusing point. "No, I mean their father. In Jackson's case, it was his mother *and* his father." She shook her head in obvious disapproval of the two she mentioned. "One worse than the other. Neither one of them deserved a kid like Jackson." The woman looked at her intently. "He's got more good in his little finger than both of them have in their entire bodies put together." Finished, Miss Joan looked at her pointedly. "Anything else?"

Feeling as if she was being skewered, Kim tried not to sound rattled as she pressed on, even though it was hard not to be. "What about the Healing Ranch?"

Miss Joan pursed her lips. "What about the Healing Ranch?"

Kim had just hoped for some free association if nothing else, but that was obviously not going to happen, so she gave the older woman a little nudge. "Do you have any feelings about that?"

Miss Joan surprised her by snorting. "Yeah, it's a hell of a job to take on, straightening out kids everyone else's given up on—including the kids themselves. But Jackson feels like he owes it to the universe, because he got a second chance to do it right. So this is his way of paying it back."

"And Garrett?" Kim asked, continuing to prod.

"Why is he taking all this on himself?" If anyone could give her some insight into the subject, Kim felt confident that the outspoken woman could.

But Miss Joan didn't answer her immediately. Instead, she looked at Kim for a long moment, as if delving into *her* thoughts. And then the woman said, "Garrett's got a heart of gold and he'd do anything for Jackson, whether or not Jackson asks him to."

Kim wasn't sure what to make of the way the older woman was looking at her. She could almost *feel* Miss Joan rummaging around in her head, even though she knew that wasn't possible. In the end, she just chalked it up to Miss Joan being strangely unique, the way everyone seemed to say she was.

"So in essence, I'm going to be doing an article on two saints."

Miss Joan frowned. "I never said those boys were saints—but did you ever notice that the biggest saints started out as the biggest sinners?"

The woman, she could see, valued honesty, so Kim decided not to try to bluff her way through this. "I'm afraid I don't quite know what you mean, Miss Joan."

"You know who Saint Augustine was, girl?" the woman asked, eyeing her closely.

"I read some of his writings in college," Kim said by way of an answer, not adding that she *had* to as part of her major and that the man's collected works had all but put her to sleep on more than one occasion.

"He was an all-round carouser, womanizer—you name it, he did it. Nearly broke his poor mother's heart. But he came around, saw the error of his ways and turned himself around. So much so that he became one of his church's saints. Shows that there's hope for everyone—and that nobody's a lost cause." Kim found herself on the receiving end of a very penetrating look. "I hope I've made myself clear."

"Yes, ma'am," Kim dutifully responded, although in truth she wasn't 100 percent certain *what* the woman was driving at.

"Good."

Kim could tell that the interview was over. "If I have any more, say, *specific* questions later on, can I come and ask you?"

The same odd smile as before curved the woman's thin lips and she shrugged in response. "You can always ask," Miss Joan told her in a lofty voice that raised more questions than it answered.

But you reserve the right not to answer if you don't want to, Kim surmised. Out loud she said, "Thanks for your time."

"What did you think of the quiche you had?" Miss Joan asked, raising her voice as she purposely remained in the kitchen instead of going out to the front of the diner.

Kim turned around to face her. "You were right," she admitted without reservation. "It was to die for."

"Not in my diner, you don't," the woman warned wryly.

Out of the corner of her eye, Kim saw Miss Joan giving a slender young woman at the far side of the kitchen a thumbs-up sign.

That had to be Angel, Kim concluded. Belatedly, she realized why Miss Joan had remained in the kitchen and asked her how she had liked her meal. So that Angel could hear the compliment first hand.

The woman, Kim thought, emerging from the kitchen

beneath the watchful eyes of Miss Joan's crew, was really something else.

Maybe she'd stay in Forever and do a quick character piece on Miss Joan after she finished writing about the Healing Ranch.

It was a thought that deserved some consideration. For the first time since she had gotten the assignment, she felt excited about writing it.

Chapter Ten

Kim walked out of the kitchen and went around the counter, all while making notes in her small spiral notebook.

Engrossed in getting key words down right so that she could remember how to phrase certain thoughts later, she didn't see Garrett standing right there until she had bumped right into him.

Because he didn't take a step back quickly enough, collision was inevitable—and not entirely unpleasant, at least not to Kim's way of thinking, even though the air had almost been knocked out of her.

Had the counter stool not been to Garrett's immediate right, she would have taken him down, most likely going with him.

As it was, Garrett barely steadied himself in time. "Hold on there, Shakespeare, you've got to look where you're going."

Startled, Kim took a second or two to focus. She hadn't expected to find Garrett still here. Even so, bodily contact registered almost immediately, before her mind was even fully registering just what had happened—and with whom.

The hot sizzle gliding at lightning speed to all parts

of her torso at once told her that she'd collided with Garrett. There was no way she could have put it to the test, but she was certain that no one else's body felt quite the way his did against hers.

She had no idea *how* she knew, she just did.

Shaking herself free of what would have, at any other time, seemed like an almost ridiculous thought, Kim did her best to regain some of her composure. Embarrassed, she tried to brazen her way out of it. "What are you doing here?"

"We just had dinner together, remember?" Garrett reminded her, amused. Cocking his head, he peered into her eyes, as if he would find the answer to his question there. "Sound vaguely familiar?"

Kim struggled to hide her impatience. "I know we had dinner together, emphasis on 'had.' I just assumed that you'd go on back to the ranch, or wherever else you intended on going tonight," she added, thinking that someone who looked the way this cowboy did most likely had a girl—or two—waiting for him at that Murphy's place he'd told her about.

"You had it right the first time. I'd be headed off to the ranch," Garrett told her.

She didn't understand. "So why are you still here?" she asked again, feeling as if she was going around in circles and wondering if he was doing that on purpose to amuse himself at her expense.

"Why, to walk you back to your hotel room, of course," he told her.

There was just a little too much sincerity in Garrett's voice for her to be buying what he was saying. She liked to think that she knew an act when she saw one. "And?"

"And make sure you're safe."

Ha! Did he think she was an idiot? Kim looked at him with barely suppressed impatience. "Oh, so you're walking me to my door, is that it?" she asked as they went out of the diner.

Taking her arm, he gently turned her toward the hotel—she'd started off in the wrong direction, but he resisted saying so out loud.

"Yes."

Garrett waited to see where this round was going because it felt exactly as if they were in the ring, dancing around one another, gloves held at the ready, with her looking for an opening.

"And you're leaving me at my door?"

Garrett refrained from saying yes. Besides, he did have a little more in mind than just that. "Well, if it's all the same to you, I'd like to make sure you go into your room."

Now they were finally getting to it, she thought with triumphant satisfaction—although, if she were being completely honest here, the idea of Garrett coming into her room and spending a little more "time" with her was intriguing, not to mention tempting. "I see. And then what?"

God, did she have to feed him his lines? she couldn't help wondering. Or was that what served as foreplay for him?

"And then I go home," Garrett answered simply.

She waited, but there didn't seem to be anything else forthcoming from him.

"And that's all?" she finally asked.

The wide, muscular shoulders rose and fell in a quick noncommittal shrug. "Unless you can think of something else—or want me to take you somewhere else—yes, that's pretty much it."

He seemed serious as he said this, but she wasn't 100 percent certain she was convinced he was telling her the truth—at least not the *whole* truth. But she couldn't very well accuse him of lying, she realized—at least not until he actually made a move on her.

"Fair enough," she temporarily agreed. "And by the way, for your information," Kim felt obliged to point out, "Shakespeare was a playwright."

"Okay."

Since the cowboy didn't seem to be reacting to what she was telling him, she added an explanation of what the term meant. "Who wrote plays."

The expression on his face was not that of a man who had just been enlightened. Instead, he patiently nodded. "Still okay."

"I'm not and I don't."

That sounded like a confession to him and while he had no idea why she thought she needed to make one, he just glided right by it. His main concern was that he wanted her to feel at ease, both with Forever and with him.

"That's nothing to be ashamed of," he told her.

Exasperated, Kim rolled her eyes. "I'm not ashamed. I'm trying to show you the difference between us."

The expression on his face told her she had officially lost him. "How's that again?"

"The difference between Shakespeare and me," she said pronouncing each word very slowly.

Garrett laughed. "That's simple enough. He's dead and you're not."

Maybe he *was* dense, Kim thought with a pronounced

sigh. "I'm referring to the fact that you called me Shakespeare."

"You're still not dead," he told her as if that was all that was being mistaken here.

She opened her mouth and then shut it again. Coming to an abrupt halt on the narrow sidewalk, she suddenly whirled around on Garrett. "You're having fun with me, aren't you?"

Not the way I'd like to, he couldn't help thinking, his mind momentarily straying to a very different definition of the word *fun*.

In response to her indignant accusation, he held up his thumb and forefinger, keeping the two apart about an inch.

"Maybe just a little," he allowed. Then, dropping his hand, Garrett continued, "Like I told you before, we don't get much by way of entertainment around here. And I called you Shakespeare because he was the first great writer we got to learn about back in school. In case I didn't go about it right, what I was doing was paying you a compliment."

"Oh." He had just taken the proverbial wind out of her sails. She looked at him, chagrined. "I didn't know," she admitted.

"Then I guess it wasn't much of a compliment," Garrett said.

Kim started to laugh then, and continued to laugh until all the tension, all the uncertainty that had been plaguing her here and over the years, was gone—at least for now.

"Did I say something funny?" Garrett enjoyed the sound of her laughter, but it did leave him feeling somewhat confused.

"No, actually you said something very sweet." That was, by her count, the second really nice thing the cowboy had said to her today, the first being that he thought she could be an investigative journalist. The man came across as if he thought more of her than she thought of herself.

And that gave her something to *really* think about.

"Thank you," she told him after a beat.

Then, with one hand on his shoulder to help brace herself, Kim rose up on her toes and impulsively brushed her lips against his cheek.

Just for a second, everything felt as if it had just stopped dead to Garrett. He considered himself—and to a large extent *was*—a great deal more experienced than Jackson. Jackson had seen the dark, dangerous side of the small Native American world around them, while he, Garrett, had garnered his experience in the world dealing with the softer sex. Because of that, he shouldn't have had this intense a reaction to something as routinely simple as an innocent kiss—and on his cheek no less, for heaven's sake. He'd moved on from that back when he was ten.

Yet here he was, with warm feelings flashing through him like lightning bugs on parade through a June night sky.

"You're welcome," he said belatedly.

All the while he was silently calling himself an idiot for reacting this way to something he would have viewed as almost hopelessly juvenile just a couple of days ago.

He was a grown man, creeping up on thirty in less than another couple of years, not some wet-behind-the ears preteen dreaming of his first serious encounter with a girl.

As they walked into the hotel lobby together, he realized he should be wary of this woman.

He'd endured worse hardships.

GARRETT WAS, by no definition or stretch of the imagination, a morning person. He never had been. He and mornings did not get along, especially when he first opened his eyes.

Most mornings he just shut them again.

And again.

And again, determined to ignore the fact that he was supposed to be getting up, and with luck, hoping he'd be falling back asleep again with only a minimum of effort.

The whole process of getting out of bed, and getting washed and dressed was one that he had had difficulty committing to no matter how many mornings he'd done it before. The thought of sleeping to noon and beyond had a seductive allure for him, even though he had never actually managed to do it.

That didn't change the fact that he aspired to it.

But this morning, Garrett made sure that he woke up earlier than he needed to and got ready.

Today was going to be Kim's first full day on the ranch and he wanted to get everything set for the young woman's arrival.

There was another reason for this uncharacteristic early rising, as well. He knew Jackson had done the bulk of everything around the ranch yesterday and was prepared to repeat it all again today. Which was why he wanted to see to a few things that needed doing before he went into Forever to pick Kim up. He owed Jackson more than a little allegiance for all the times his brother had put himself between his father's belt and his own thin body.

The last words Kim had said to him before closing her hotel door was that she was perfectly capable of driving herself over to the ranch now that she knew the way. Given what he had witnessed regarding her poor sense of direction, he'd told her that he intended to be there to pick her up all the same.

And he had meant it. But he still needed to take care of a couple of things here at the ranch.

He stepped up his pace.

"WHAT ARE YOU doing up?" Jackson asked in complete stunned surprise when he saw his brother walking into the kitchen twenty minutes before seven.

It was at least an hour before they all—and that included the boys who were currently staying and working at the ranch—gathered at the dining room table for breakfast.

Garrett paused by the kitchen counter. "It's a new day, Jackson, and I intend to meet it head on," he told his brother with a purposely guileless grin as he poured himself a cup of coffee. He took it black and fairly strong. He sampled some before continuing. It was strong enough to open up all the pores of his body and have them stand up and salute. "This is really good coffee, Debi."

Turning toward his sister-in-law, he raised his cup in a mock toast. Rosa, their newly hired all-around housekeeper, made the meals for all of them, but Debi was in charge of the coffee. Since joining the household, she'd quickly become an expert at it, making it strong enough to please Jackson, yet not strong enough to burn out the lining of their stomachs the way Jackson's version of coffee had threatened to do on a daily basis.

Jackson set down his own cup of coffee and eyed him. Garrett normally wasn't conscious enough to comment on anything, much less dispense with a compliment. "Okay, who are you and what have you done with my brother?"

"I am who I've always been, Jackson," Garrett answered.

Coffee cup in one hand, he made his way around the stove, managing to steal one strip of bacon from the first of the three batches that Rosa always prepared for their breakfast.

Rosa swatted his hand, issuing him a warning in free-flowing Spanish. The fact that she couldn't quite hide her smile took some of the sting out of the warning.

Jackson laughed shortly in response to his brother's answer. "Not hardly."

"Leave him alone, Jackson," Debi said. "Can't you see he's happy?" Turning toward her brother-in-law, she asked, "Do you want me to make you a quick breakfast on the side before you go? Rosa's busy and I've got time before the clinic opens."

The clinic, still relatively in its infancy, now boasted two nurses in addition to its two doctors. Like everyone else on the staff, Debi put in long hours, and even if he had been starving, Garrett would have refused to give her more work than she was already handling.

So he shook his head. "Not hungry, Deb. And if I suddenly *do* get hungry I can always grab something at Miss Joan's."

"You can save yourself some money by eating here," Jackson told him, then added in an offhanded manner, "You can feed that writer of yours here, too, if you want."

Managing to cover up his surprise, Garrett said, "Thanks for the offer."

Jackson was a generous man, Garret thought, but he knew that his brother drew the line at people he had no use for, especially those who got paid for poking around in his life. The fact that Jackson had told him to bring Kim back to the house for breakfast was actually a pretty big deal for his brother.

"But she's not my writer," Garrett pointed out.

Jackson looked up and his eyes met Garrett's. "If you say so," he muttered. "Bring her back and feed her, anyway. She's already coming to the ranch to ask questions and there's no need for you to throw away your money if you don't have to."

Stealing a second piece of bacon, this time behind Rosa's back, Garrett began to walk out of the kitchen, headed for the front door.

"I'm going to go look in on Wicked first before I go," he told Jackson. Draining his coffee, he left the cup on the first flat surface he passed.

"Good idea," Jackson called after him. "The palomino's forgetting what you look like."

Instead of engaging in any further discussion regarding the stallion—or anything else for that matter—Garrett just raised his hand and waved it without turning around or even looking over his shoulder at his brother. He just kept on walking until he had left the house.

Debi turned to her husband. "Jackson, don't ride your brother like that," she told him.

Jackson shrugged innocently. "Hell, it's a dirty job, but someone's got to do it." In a fluid movement, he leaned forward and snagged her by the waistband of her jeans, pulling her right onto his lap and into his arms. "Speaking of dirty jobs," he went on, looking at her with a deliberate leer on his face.

Debi pretended to take offense. She braced her hands against his chest to maintain a small wedge of space between them.

"Well, I like that," she huffed.

To which Jackson grinned in response. "I certainly hope so," he told her just before he bent his head down to share what he regarded to be a brief, but life-affirming kiss.

When he was done, he drew his head back slowly, as well as reluctantly. Getting to his feet, he still kept his arms around Debi as she stood up beside him.

The rest of the day was still waiting to unfold, but he hated being separated from Debi, even for the space of a workday. He loved her fiercely and he wasn't ashamed to admit it to anyone who would listen.

How the hell did one man manage to get so lucky? he wondered, feeling extremely grateful that this woman had come into his life.

Looking up at her husband, Debi tightened her arms around his neck.

"I *do* like that," she repeated, saying the same words she'd uttered a moment ago, plus one more, but with a much different emphasis now.

Jackson's grin grew deeper as he lingered a little longer, reveling in the warmth he felt emanating from her body. He couldn't remember ever feeling this alive, or this happy.

"Good," he repeated. "Me, too," he told her just before indulging in another long, soulful kiss.

Chapter Eleven

Garrett arrived at the hotel early.

Kim was even earlier.

The fact that she was ready on time, much less ready early, surprised the cowboy to the point of near disbelief.

For the most part, the women he knew or had dealings with, other than possibly his mother and Debi, were all notoriously late. "On time" in their world took in a broad range of time and they were anywhere from a few minutes late to two hours late. He had gotten used to that sort of interpretation.

But when he arrived at Kim's door, wanting only to tell her that he would be in the lobby, he was surprised to see Kim open it at the very first sound of his voice.

"Ready," she announced with a hint of breathlessness as she closed the last button on her long-sleeve, light blue blouse. She grabbed her jacket and pulled the door closed behind her.

Garrett automatically let his eyes sweep over her and he couldn't help thinking that he should be the one who was breathless, not her.

Not that he wasn't struggling with just that right now.

The button she had just fastened was making a bid

for freedom and looked set to uncouple itself from the buttonhole that was supposed to contain it. He found himself rooting for the button.

With effort, he raised his eyes to Kim's face.

"You didn't have to hurry," he told her.

They walked to the elevator at the end of the hall. She pressed the Down button before turning to him. "I could say the same thing to you."

"What makes you think I hurried?" he asked, wondering what could have possibly given him away.

He'd carefully looked himself over before he'd left his room, making sure that he was presentable and there was nothing about him—as far as he could tell—to suggest that he had ramped up his usual time getting ready and driving into town.

As a rule, he *didn't* hurry, but it had seemed worth it today.

Getting into the elevator, she told him, "One of the people I talked to about Jackson and you yesterday mentioned that you were the brother who liked to sleep in."

Garrett avoided her eyes as they got off the elevator and headed toward the hotel's front door. "Nobody sleeps in on a ranch. Things have to get done early."

He just didn't bother expanding on that, or telling her that he'd had to get up early in order to do what he felt obligated to take care of before he drove into Forever.

"Sounds exhausting," she commented.

The sun seemed extrabright as she and Garrett walked out of the hotel and she shaded her eyes as she looked around the immediate area. The town wasn't bustling, but given the small level of activity, it was definitely awake.

His shrug was casual. "It has its rewards. Are you hungry?"

He figured that was more or less a rhetorical question since he assumed that she was. On the way into town he had already decided to take her to Miss Joan's before they headed back to the ranch despite what Jackson had said.

"As a matter of fact, I'm stuffed." When he looked at her, she realized that she'd left out one critical piece of information. "Miss Joan had one of her waitresses bring over a tray of food to my hotel room. She said that she thought I should be 'fortified,' I think the word she used was, for what lay ahead. I was kind of surprised," she confessed. "I thought the hotel didn't have room service."

"They don't," he told her. Arriving where his truck was parked by the hotel entrance, he held the passenger-side door opened for her. "Miss Joan made an exception for you."

Sitting down, she waited until Garrett was in on his side before asking, "Why?"

He pushed the metal tongue into the seat belt slot, automatically listening for it to click into place. "Because she's Miss Joan and she does things like that. People around here know better than to question her on it." He spared Kim a smile before starting up his vehicle. "We just say thank-you and move along."

Kim couldn't help making a comparison between the people in Forever and her neighborhood in San Francisco. It really was another world out here, she thought.

"She's a very exceptional woman," Kim told him.

He merely laughed quietly in response as they left Forever. "That she is."

DURING THEIR DRIVE to the ranch, she used the time to ask Garrett a multitude of questions. Some were strictly routine, run-of-the-mill questions. Others were far more probing and unique to the programs offered at the Healing Ranch. What she was trying to get at was how the ranch was still being operated as a ranch, yet also as a specialized rehabilitation center.

Garrett answered her questions as best he could and for her part, she took his replies down word for word, writing them all into her slightly worn notebook.

"I don't think I've ever seen anyone write that fast," Garrett told her when they finally drove onto the ranch.

Since the road was wide-open, he glanced at the pad, expecting to see nothing but uneven rows of chicken scratch. Instead, he was surprised when even in motion, he could make out every word.

"It's legible," he declared in surprise.

"And why wouldn't it be?"

He started to explain. "I thought because you wrote so fast—never mind," he said, giving up and feeling a little foolish—as well as impressed that she could move her pen across the page so quickly and not be sloppy or messy about it.

When he'd met her, he'd thought that she was somewhat scattered, but now he realized that she was anything but. Despite the fact that for the most part he was laidback, he had always admired someone who was organized in the face of chaos—the way, he now supposed, that Jackson had become.

"Where would you like to start?" he asked Kim as he drove up to the ranch house.

Removing her seat belt, she shifted so that she was

able to face him as she replied, "Anywhere you want me to."

He really wished that she would stop feeding him loaded lines like that. One of these times, he was going to say the first thing that came to his mind and it wouldn't go well for him after that.

Or maybe it would, a small voice in his head whispered, playing devil's advocate.

He deliberately blocked it and focused only on the reason why Kim was here and not on the woman herself. "We can start by introducing you to the ranch hands."

"The boys you're working with," she said just to be sure they were talking about the same people.

"One and the same," Garrett told her, nodding his head.

There was an early-morning breeze threading its way around the area and it ruffled his hair. She found herself wanting to do the same.

Kim pressed her hands to her sides as they cut across to the corral.

HAVING BEEN FOREWARNED regarding the nature of her work and that she was going to be around for a few days, the boys were prepared for Kim's appearance this time around. Consequently, they were all respectful and a little less wary than they had been the day before.

Jackson had remained in the background like a silent, protective force, his presence acutely felt if not actually heard.

Kim made sure to acknowledge him.

"I'd like to talk to each of them when you're finished with them," she said to Jackson. The last thing she wanted to do was to tread on his toes or disrupt any of his routines.

"I won't be 'finished' with them until they're ready to go home," Jackson informed her quietly, but there was no mistaking the fact that he had taken exception to the way she had worded her request.

Kim flushed, but still held her ground rather than backing off. "I meant finished for the day."

"I can't tell you when that'll be," he said honestly. "They work for their keep, so it's an ongoing process."

Kim suggested a compromise. "When they get a break, then." She turned her back to Jackson and lowered her voice as she enlisted Garrett's help. "Tell your brother I'm on his side, that I'm just trying to get this down right so that people can see what the two of you are accomplishing here." Still, she knew she couldn't just keep butting her head against a stone wall. "If he really doesn't want me to write the story—"

"He does, he does. He just needs more coffee, that's all." Garrett decided that it was best to level with her so that she knew exactly why his brother was behaving like this. "I think he's worried that no matter what you see here, you'll do a hatchet job on the ranch once you write this all up."

She stared at him, dumbfounded. "Why would I do that?"

"Because he knows that something on the more exciting or underhanded side will sell more copies," Garrett suggested pointedly.

He was referring to her question about making more money if they were operating a casino, she realized.

"Probably," she allowed, then surprised him by saying, "But I'm not about to lie in print to sell more copies.

I'm just here to put the truth down on paper, whatever that turns out to be."

She turned back to Jackson. The latter had already moved on and was instructing a group of teens who were clustered around him. "Tell you what," she said, raising her voice as she crossed over to the older brother, "how about this? I give you my final copy for you to okay. You don't like it, it doesn't get sent in."

"Can't get any fairer than that," Garrett pointed out to his brother.

"Guess not." Jackson's sky-blue eyes shifted over to his brother. "When you're done writing, give it to Garrett to read. If it's okay with him, it's okay with me."

Garrett laughed, shaking his head. "He just doesn't like to read," he told her.

"And he doesn't like any extra work," Jackson countered, nodding at his brother. "Or to work at all for that matter."

Kim smiled to herself as she looked from one brother to the other. She had a feeling she had just found the angle she'd been looking for.

Two days of intensive work later, each amounting to more than eighteen hours at a clip, Kim was reasonably certain that the end was in sight. She had even checked in twice with Stan to keep the editor apprised of the article's development.

The piece, though admittedly far from exciting, was coming along. She had managed to infuse just enough upbeat enthusiasm in her article to engage the reader—or so she hoped.

As she reviewed the article again for the fourth time,

she knew that it was a pretty tame piece. Kim frowned at it thoughtfully.

Punching it up began to consume her, laying siege to all her thoughts and everything she was doing. Which was why she didn't see it coming until it was too late. Didn't see what would, when she looked back at the incident later, completely change the direction of her life.

Didn't see that same life being threatened as one moment she was just walking back to her car parked in front of the ranch house—she'd driven herself to the ranch today—to get something out of the trunk, the next moment, before she knew it, Garrett was racing over to her, yelling, "Get out of the way!"

Not waiting for his order to register or for her to react to it, Garrett acted on it.

Kim barely had time to turn in the direction of his voice before she found herself being thrown to the ground with Garrett's body right on top of hers.

Any spontaneous reaction that might have been accompanied by an indignant protest or outraged query regarding the state of his mind and if he had lost it, vanished almost before it could materialize. Vanished because the reason for Garrett's sudden completely unexpected dive over her body became instantly apparent to her.

Horses' hooves galloped by, missing her head, now on the ground, by inches.

Besides the galloping hooves pounding the ground, there were more noises around her: the sound of voices shouting at one another, and cries of concern and fear all blending together.

But as many as there were, they were all well in the background, barely registering.

What absorbed the bulk of her attention was the feel of Garrett's body on hers.

Pressing on hers.

Blending with hers.

It seemed to Kim that time had somehow stopped, freezing in place as their eyes met and held in an eternal moment.

All sorts of feelings she couldn't begin to identify and label were bursting through her like some massive holiday light show.

The sound, or rather the *feel* of running feet coming closer echoed in her chest, amplifying her pounding heart and her racing pulse.

Resonating through every inch of her like some primal concerto.

"Are you all right?" Garrett was asking as he scrambled off her and pulled himself into a sitting position beside her. His eyes were sweeping over her, not in admiration but in total concern.

Shaken, she pulled herself up into a sitting position. It took her a second to process his question.

"Yes, I think so. What just happened?" she asked, still bewildered.

"Jordy lost control of his horse and for some reason, the mare got spooked and took off. He was running after the horse, trying to grab the reins and that just spooked her even more. Flower was coming right at you," he told her solemnly.

"Flower?" she repeated, the word just not registering with her brain.

"The mare. Her name is Flower." Already on his feet, Garrett held out his hand to her when he saw her trying to stand up. "Here, let me help you up."

He didn't wait for Kim to hold out her hand, instead, he took it and began to gently pull her to her feet. The gasp of sheer pain that escaped her lips had him stopping immediately. Instinctively, he lowered her back to the ground.

"I guess maybe I'm not all right," she said, completely stunned by the pain she'd just felt searing through her. For a second, at a loss for thoughts, Kim looked accusingly at her right leg. The pain was originating from there.

"What hurts?" he asked her as a gaggle of teenage boys began gathering around them.

"I'm not sure." But the sharp spear of pain that shot through her as she tried to move her foot narrowed it down considerably. "It's my ankle, I think," she said, struggling to keep the pain at bay. "I must have turned it."

"Or worse," Jackson speculated as he came forward. Standing in front of the teens he was overseeing, he looked around now for an explanation. "What happened here?"

A disjointed symphony of voices all began talking at once, trying to answer him. Kim raised her own voice so that it was louder than the others. Despite what Garrett had just told her, she wasn't about to point fingers.

"I just tripped," she told Jackson, flashing a contrite smile in his direction. "Sorry."

But Jackson and Garrett had impressed all their charges about the importance of telling the truth and the need for clear consciences.

"My horse got loose, sir," a tall, gangly boy with dark brown eyes and a sallow complexion spoke up, coming forward. This had to be the Jordy that Garrett had referred to, Kim thought. "I'm sorry. I guess I'm not ready to train my own horse yet."

"We'll talk later," Jackson told him. "I'll call my wife," he said to Kim, "and ask her to come out to take a look at that." He nodded at her leg. "Garrett, take some of the boys and catch Jordy's horse before she makes it all the way to Mexico."

"It's okay, don't bother your wife. I don't want to disrupt anything," Kim told him, catching hold of Jackson's sleeve. "I just need to stay off it for a little while."

"You probably do," Garrett agreed. Taking out his keys, he tossed them to one of the boys who was over sixteen. "Adam, open up my truck for me. Leave the keys in the ignition. Sorry, Jackson, someone else is going to have to lead the chase for Flower."

The next second, Garrett squatted down beside her and scooped Kim up off the ground. Amused by the surprised look on her face, he rose to his feet.

"You can stay off it in my truck. You're going into town," he told her. "I'm taking you to the clinic to see one of the doctors."

"I'll be all right," she protested again even as Garrett began walking to his vehicle.

"And I'm going to make sure that you are," he told her in a firm tone that told her there was no point in her trying to argue with him.

Jackson was already taking out his cell phone. "I'll call Debi and tell her you're coming," he said, calling out after his brother.

"I'd appreciate it," Garrett replied without turning around.

"I can probably walk, or at least hobble to the car," she insisted. She felt awkward about having to be carried to the vehicle. In part it ate into her self-image. A person in control of their situation didn't need to be carried.

"Like hell you will," he informed her, making no effort to put her down. "You can't walk or hobble if your ankle's broken."

That he wasn't elaborating on the best possible scenario surprised her. "Since when are you not an optimist?" she asked.

The man she had gotten to know over these past few days—and become extremely attracted to, as well—was a complete optimist with nothing but unending faith and hope when it came to the ranch and to his brother. This was totally out of character for him. What was going on here?

"Caution has always been the better part of valor," was all he said as he brought her to his truck.

Chapter Twelve

"How are you doing?"

Garrett slanted a quick look at the woman he had gently placed into the passenger seat of his truck before taking off, hell-for-leather, for Forever and the medical clinic.

He kept his eyes on the road ahead. The last thing he wanted to do was hit an uneven patch, rattling the truck and causing Kim even more pain. She hadn't complained—hadn't said much of anything, really—but she was a great deal paler than normal and that was making him uneasy.

"The same as when you asked me a couple of minutes ago," Kim answered, slowly measuring out her words. "And a couple of minutes before that."

All through her childhood, both of her parents had always made it plain that they wouldn't tolerate complaining. That in turn had taught her, early on, the meaning of the phrase *grin and bear it*. Moaning and carrying on not only wasn't accepted in her family, it was highly frowned upon. In time, she grew to have the same opinion.

She wasn't about to change course now.

"That has to hurt a lot," he commented, trying to draw her out.

It did, but what was the point in saying so? Because of her upbringing, her instinctive reaction was to look down on anyone who whined if they were over the age of ten.

Kim shrugged, staring out through the windshield at the road. "It could be worse."

"Hell, it could always be worse," he granted, "but it could be a lot better, too."

Saying that, he pressed down even harder on the gas pedal. Maybe she was slipping into some kind of a delirious state and was being delusional. He wanted to get her to the clinic before it got any worse.

Kim suddenly sucked in air as a fresh sharp pain slashed through her.

"I'll be fine," she insisted, still not looking at him. She gripped the right armrest next to her, as if that would somehow help her balance out the pain or maybe even channel it.

It didn't.

Garrett caught the movement out of the corner of his eye, heard the momentary unguarded noise escape her lips. "You sure? Want me to get you a stick to bite on?"

Sweat was popping out on her brow. Kim pressed her lips together as she tried to come to terms with the pain emanating from her throbbing ankle.

Just a little farther, she promised herself. *Just a little farther and the pain'll be gone.*

She was clenching her teeth, trying to project herself past the pain. It wasn't working all that well. "I'm just peachy," she breathed.

"Well, 'Peachy,' we're here," Garrett announced,

coming to an abrupt stop right in front of the clinic. The second the brake was on, he hopped out of the cab and rounded the hood to get to her side.

"Aren't you in the way of traffic, parking like this?" Kim asked, looking around.

Garrett snorted. "This is Forever, there is no traffic."

"But—"

Getting her into the clinic was his first priority, everything else was taking second place. As gently as he could under the circumstances, he lifted her out of his truck.

"I'll park it better later," he promised. "First, we get you inside."

"If you put one arm around my waist, I could try to walk," she told him. She didn't want him to keep carrying her around like this. She wasn't *that* light.

He made no effort to even attempt to see if her suggestion worked. Instead, he just walked to the clinic's front steps. "Man, but you are the bossiest woman I have ever run into."

She knew it was useless to argue with him, especially in this position. And she had to admit that she did like having him carry her like this.

Kim stopped resisting.

Now that she thought about it, this tied into a fantasy she'd had as a little girl. She was rather fuzzy on the details, but she remembered that it had something to do with being rescued from a fire-breathing dragon by a fearless, handsome prince. At the time, the prince had had blond hair, but she wasn't a stickler. Garrett suited her fantasy just fine.

"You're grinning," he noted as he walked up the

three front steps to the clinic. He looked at her a little uncertainly. "Should I be concerned?"

No, but maybe I should.

She shook her head in response to his question. "I was just thinking of something."

"What?"

Kim flushed slightly. Just then, the clinic's front door opened and Debi was standing in the doorway. This was *not* the time to talk about princes and fantasies, she thought.

"I'll tell you later," she promised Garrett.

Debi opened the door all the way. "Dr. Davenport's with a patient, but Dr. Cordell will see you in exam room two," Debi told her, squeezing Kim's hand and offering her a warm smile that promised she'd be fine very soon.

And then the clinic's newest nurse turned to look at Garrett. "It's not nice to break outsiders, Garrett, you know that. What did you do to her?"

Kim answered for him before Garrett even had the chance. "What he did was saved me from being trampled by a horse."

Since Garrett was carrying the woman in his arms, Debi looked over her lower extremities quickly. The ankle was already swollen and appeared to be getting worse.

"So you trampled her instead?" she asked, glancing back at Garrett.

Garrett slanted his sister-in-law a glance and shook his head. "You've been spending too much time with Jackson."

"No," Debi told him as she led the way into the back

of the clinic and then to the second exam room, "not enough, I'm afraid."

From her vantage point in Garrett's arms, Kim could see that the waiting room was pretty much filled up. This was apparently a regular state of affairs, given that it had been like that when she'd come in to talk to the doctors the other day. At the time she'd come to briefly interview each on their take on the Healing Ranch and the two men who ran it.

Now, of course, it was different. Now she wasn't here as a working writer; she was here as an injured patient in need of medical attention.

She didn't like being in this sort of a position.

And she had never been one who felt that what or who she was, or who her parents were, gave her the right to arbitrarily go to the head of the line. That was especially true now, even though her ankle was beginning to hurt like crazy.

She bit her lip for a second, trying to come to terms with the pain before continuing.

"Shouldn't all these people go first?" she asked Garrett's sister-in-law. "They were here ahead of me," she added needlessly.

"When Garrett called, I told them about your accident and they took a vote," Debi told her, clearing the old paper off the exam table and putting down a new sheet on it. "You can put her down now," she told Garrett.

"Seriously?" Kim asked, still trying to come to terms with what the nurse had just told her. She wasn't really sure if she believed Debi or not.

Debi flashed her a smile as she got everything in order for the doctor's examination. "Seriously. You came just at the right time. Nobody in the waiting room's been injured, so they all opted for you to go in first."

Kim looked past Garrett's shoulder toward the waiting room. Even though there was a wall up in between them, she could still visualize the people sitting out there.

"Well, this is a first," she murmured.

"Not around here," Debi told her brightly, then leaned in to add in a lowered voice, "But I know what you mean. I'm from a bigger city, too. Not as big as San Francisco, but big enough to lose a town like Forever in," she told Kim with a wink. Straightening again, she turned to look at her brother-in-law. "Why don't you come on out to the waiting room, and I'll come and get you when the doctor's finished."

Garrett appeared surprised at her suggestion. "I kind of thought that I'd just hang around here, with Kim," he told Debi.

His sister-in-law's response to that was to point to the door. "I'm afraid you thought wrong, honey. You need to wait in the waiting room."

Garrett took a couple of steps toward the door, then stopped and stood just shy of the threshold. He eyed Kim, reluctant to leave her like this. "You'll be all right?" he asked her.

"She'll be perfect," his sister-in-law assured him. Putting her hands against his back, she gave him a gentle push out of the room. "Now go."

"I'll go," he told Debi. "But I won't like it."

"Guess I can't have everything," Debi responded philosophically. She fastened the blood pressure cuff around Kim's right arm and proceeded to take a reading. The numbers were just perfect. "Looks like being around Garrett and the boys hasn't had any ill effects on you," Debi noted, making a notation of the reading on the chart. "Dr. C. will be in shortly." She paused, looking into Kim's eyes. The woman's blood pressure might have been right on target, but she was definitely tense. "Can I get you anything?"

Kim thought of Garrett's comment about getting her a stick to bite on. She was even closer to that point now than before, but she told herself that she could tough it out for a few more minutes—with just a little bit more luck.

She shook her head in response to Debi's question. "I'm okay."

Debi watched her for a long moment. "Tell your teeth that." When Kim raised her eyebrow in a silent question, she elaborated, "You clench them any harder and you're liable to crack them right in half. I'll ask the doctor if it's okay to give you a shot of hydrocodone to help with the pain."

She recognized the name of the painkiller. That, she knew, was liable to make her drowsy, and she had work to do, notes to organize and the article to continue whipping into shape.

She still had things she wanted to get down, but writing the third, longer draft was not that far away. She couldn't do any of that if she was drowsy. "I really don't think—"

"No, that's the doctor's job," Debi told her. "That's what you're paying her for." Finished, she wrapped up the blood pressure cuff and returned it to its rightful place against the wall. With that, she moved to the doorway. "The doctor'll be right here," Debi promised and then closed the door.

Kim settled back, doing her best to ignore the stabbing pain.

The doctor'll be right here.

She knew what that meant. The doctor would be in the room sometime shortly before the second coming. Possibly even at the same time.

Still, she supposed she had no other choice but to wait here and—

When the door opened again less than a minute later, Kim looked up, startled.

"Did you forget something?" she asked, thinking that Garrett's sister-in-law had returned to the exam room for some reason.

"Not that I know of, but I am getting a little scattered at times, juggling patients and that new husband of mine." Dr. Cordell laughed as she closed the door behind her.

Feeling a little embarrassed, Kim apologized. "Oh, I'm sorry, I thought you were Debi."

One hand back on the doorknob, Alisha Cordell was ready to step out in the hall and call for Debi to come back into the room. "Did you need to see her?"

"Oh, no, thank you," Kim added as an afterthought. "I just thought you were her. I mean, I didn't expect to see you so soon." This wasn't coming out right, she chastised herself.

"I can go back outside and make an entrance in slow motion if you'd like." Alisha deadpanned. And then she laughed and waved her hand at her patient when she saw Kim struggling to attempt to make some sort of coherent, serious reply.

"I know, the pace around here takes a little getting used to. Fast, but still with the proper amount of concern. I don't mind telling you that this is a lot different than the kind of doctoring I thought I'd be doing—and *was* doing back in New York.

"So," she continued, switching back into her doctor mode, "I've already been filled in, but why don't you give me your take on what happened," Alisha encouraged, moving closer to her patient.

Succinctly, Kim did just that. She filled the doctor in on the collision and the aftermath while Alisha was giving her a general exam to make sure there were no other injuries beyond the obvious one.

There weren't.

Then she went on to the injured ankle, carefully testing its range of motion and assessing the extent of the damage.

"This, mercifully, looks a lot worse than it actually is, but I won't lie to you," Alisha said, completing the exam and calling for two splints, one to be applied to either side of the ankle before it was bound tightly up. "It's going to hurt like a son of a gun for the first forty-eight hours."

"Forty-eight hours?" Kim echoed, distressed. Up until a couple of hours ago, she had been secretly lamenting that she was going to have to be leaving the ranch—and Garrett—all too soon. Now she found herself having trouble coming to terms with *not* leaving. "But I'm supposed to be in San Francisco by then."

"Family obligations?" Alisha asked, carefully wrapping the bandage tightly around the splints.

Kim shook her head.

"Magazine obligations." She had long since gotten

out of the general family loop. She still loved her parents and sisters, but she kept that part of her life under wraps. To allude to it was cause for embarrassment, so she had stopped focusing on the holidays as a time for gatherings and instead thought of it as a time to get in some extensive shopping.

Except that was off the table, now because of her stupid ankle.

"I've got an article due."

"Ah, yes, that one you said you were working on," Alisha recalled. "Well, you can email it to them," she suggested. "My advice to you is to take it easy for at least a week or so, stay off your foot it as much as possible. And no undue stress," she warned.

Kim had almost stopped listening to the rest of it when she'd heard what the doctor said initially. "A week?" she questioned, trying to bank down her distress.

"Or so," Alisha added again. Taking pity on Kim, she made her an offer. "I can call whoever you need me to and tell them that in my professional opinion, you could do a lot of damage to that ankle if you're not careful. The next week, or better yet two, are crucial." Alisha must have seen the mounting alarm on her patient's face. "If you give me your magazine's phone number—"

But Kim shook her head. "No, that won't be necessary. You don't need to call anyone. I was just thinking that this just kind of messes up some of my plans," she explained to the doctor.

Alisha nodded. "I know what you mean. Life has a habit of doing that to us, messing up perfectly good plans. But you know, there's an old saying that there's nothing so bad that some good can't come out of it." She smiled. "When we both have time, I can tell you how I personally found that to be very, very true."

She took out her prescription pad and made a quick notation before writing them out. "Now, here's a prescription for some antibiotics to make sure that that area doesn't get infected, and here's another for painkillers." She tore them off one at a time. "I can give you a concentrated shot to start you off if you're in a lot of pain."

Even though she was still in more than a fair amount of pain, she wanted to remain clearheaded. "I can handle it."

"I had a feeling," Alisha said, putting her prescription pad away in her oversize lab coat pocket. There was a knock on the door behind her. "Oh, one more thing," Alisha said as the door opened and the other nurse, Holly, came in. The latter was carrying a set of crutches. "I know how hard it is to stay completely off your feet, so these should help you when you absolutely, positively need to move around."

Holly set the crutches down, leaning them against the wall and then silently withdrawing. Neither woman saw the wary way Kim eyed the crutches.

"Okay, if you don't have any questions for me," Alisha went on, "let me go tell Garrett you're ready to leave. He's outside, pacing around like a man who's about to jump out of his skin at any second. He's really worried about you," she added. "See if you can reassure him," she said with a wink just before she left the room.

Chapter Thirteen

The moment the door to the exam room closed, Kim focused on the crutches. Pressing her lips together to stifle any unintentional exclamations of pain, she slid over to one side of the exam table, going as far as she could.

The crutches were leaning against the wall directly opposite to where she was sitting. Supporting her weight as best she could with her left hand, Kim began to wiggle forward until her feet—or actually just her left foot—touched the floor. There was no way she could put any weight on her right foot so this, perforce, was going to be a balancing act.

Leaning forward from that vantage point, she finally managed to hook her fingers around the crutches and pull them to her. With the exam table against the small of her back, she took a crutch in each hand and only then did she even try to stand up.

The cry of pain was involuntary and burst out despite her attempt to keep her lips pressed shut. She all but collapsed against the exam table, which was still at her back.

Garrett opened the door just in time to see what happened. He cut the distance between them down to nothing in less than half a heartbeat.

"What are you trying to do?" he cried as he pulled her upright and against him.

"I was *trying* to stand up," she said angrily.

The anger that burst out had nothing to do with him or his question, or even the embarrassment she felt that he had seen her fail this way. It was mainly directed at herself and it echoed with her frustration.

"Maybe it's just too soon to try that. Give it some time," he suggested. In Kim's place, he probably would have done the same thing. But being in *his* place, he could also see the futility in pushing too hard so quickly.

But she frowned, looking at the crutches angrily. "There's never going to be a right time for that." She raised her eyes to his, acutely aware that his arms were still around her. She felt as if she was engaged in a two-front war. Fighting for her independence and fighting the desire just to give in and melt into his arms. "I can't use crutches."

His smile was understanding and encouraging. For a second, she wanted to double up her fists and beat on his chest. The next moment, she was fighting the urge to bury her head in it and sob.

"Everybody probably has trouble at first," he told her. "It's got to feel awkward trying to—"

"No," Kim cut him off. He didn't understand, she thought, exasperated. "I *can't* use crutches." She *hated* talking about her shortcomings, but he was waiting for her to explain. "I tore three out of four of the muscles in my rotor cuff in my right shoulder. The surgery to repair it would have put me out of commission for a long time and I'd just gotten started writing for a couple of the bigger magazines, so I opted for physical therapy."

The routine had been grueling, but she'd wanted to

get back to work as soon as possible. To her, it had been worth every agonizing moment.

"It helped and I can almost do everything I used to, but that shoulder is definitely weaker and what that means, in my case, anyway, is that I can't use my shoulder to support part of my weight when I'm on crutches—so I can't use the crutches."

He saw the tears in her eyes as she spoke. He had come to know her well enough now to understand those tears were neither a ploy for sympathy nor tears of self-pity. If anything, they were just the outward manifestation of her inner frustration. He deliberately pretended not to notice them so that she could keep her dignity.

Moving the crutches aside, he said, "We'll figure something out," and then he lifted her into his arms.

"You can't keep carrying me around like this," she protested.

"Everyone's entitled to have one fantasy come true," he replied, walking out of the exam room. He went past the reception desk and then into the waiting area.

"Wait," she cried, trying to twist around so she could see Holly at the reception desk. "I need to pay for the visit."

But Garrett kept right on heading for the front door. "That's already been settled up," he assured her.

"How?" She hadn't shown anyone her insurance card or her credit card. There was no way a payment had been made.

"I had Debi take care of it," Garrett answered calmly.

She wanted to protest that she could pay her own way. Wanted to tell him that he needed to turn around and go back to the reception desk so that she could do it, but she didn't want to dress him down in front of people he knew—especially when those people were now all looking at them leave the clinic. Some of those patients were even waving goodbye to her, since she was facing in their direction as Garrett carried her out.

A few called out, as well, saying they hoped she felt better.

She had no idea what to say in response so she merely waved back.

The second the clinic door closed behind them, though, she said to Garrett, "Those people don't know me from Adam. Why would they care if I feel better or not?"

The answer seemed rather obvious to him. "Because they're nice people. And just between us, I think even the simplest of them can tell you apart from any guy named 'Adam,'" he assured her.

Unable to help herself, Kim just laughed at his comment. It wound up being a full-fledged, straight-from-the-gut-until-it-almost-hurt kind of laugh. And then she just buried her face against his shoulder, hiding there or maybe just focusing on gathering some inner strength to face the rest of her ordeal.

Kim said nothing as he deposited her into the passenger seat, then very gently slid the seat belt buckle into the side slot for her.

She said nothing as he loaded the useless crutches into the back—not even to ask him why he was bothering to bring them along when she couldn't use them.

And she said nothing when he finally got into the driver's side and started up the truck.

But ten minutes into the trip, with Forever behind them, the silence finally ate away at her.

"Aren't you going to say anything?" she asked, turning as best she could to look at him. He might have buckled her up gently, but she found that the seat belt held her tightly in place.

"I thought I'd wait for you to start," Garrett responded.

She blew out a breath, more to calm herself than for any other reason. "All right, now what?" she asked. She looked down at her heavily bandaged foot and could feel her frustration growing.

"Now we see about getting you well," he replied quietly.

"Getting me well?" she repeated, her tone both bewildered and skeptical. "You mean like using some sort of Navajo magic on this?" She winced as she tried to tap the top of the bulky bandage.

"Ingenuity and patience aren't exclusive to the Navajo culture, although we have had occasion to practice a great deal of both in the last century or so," he allowed.

"I don't get it."

Garrett smiled, trying to put her at ease. "We'll try a little bit of therapy, a little bit of this and that, and see what works."

She was really hoping he had more of a plan than just those vague words. She sat back against her seat, her arms crossed in front of her to show her resigned annoyance. "Not very scientific."

He wasn't trying to be scientific. Because of where he came from, and because he had Jackson as an example, he relied much more on instinct and gut feelings.

"Well, these things never completely are," he told her.

She wanted something that worked, something to help her heal fast and get on with things.

Things.

Stan.

Her eyes widened as thoughts came colliding back to her. "But I've got to finish the article," she suddenly protested.

With everything that had happened in the past couple of hours, the reason she was in Forever in the first place had completely slipped her mind.

"There's nothing wrong with your mind or your hands," Garrett calmly pointed out, "so I suspect you'll get it done."

She looked down in angry frustration at her right foot. "If I have to stay off this, how am I supposed to drive back and forth from the hotel?"

"Simple," he replied. "You're not."

"But I can't observe you and Jackson work with those so-called 'ranch hands' so I can put that into the article if I'm at the hotel."

"No," he agreed. "You can't." Before she could start to protest again, he told her, "You're staying at the ranch. There's a small bedroom on the ground floor. You can stay there for as long as you need to. That way you can observe to your heart's content and get the article written on time."

Stay at the ranch, right, she thought sarcastically. As if that would happen. "Won't Jackson have something to say about that?"

"Sure," he agreed. "I think the word you're looking for is *yes*."

"Jackson's been polite to me, but I'm well aware that I'm not exactly his favorite person."

"No," Garrett freely agreed, "but you're growing on him. And besides," he pointed out, sparing her a glance, "you forget that Jackson's a good guy. He'd never turn out someone who couldn't stand up for themselves—literally," he threw in.

Kim shook her head. Garrett was making sense, she supposed, but that didn't alter any of the facts as she saw them.

"I don't feel right about this," she told him.

If that was all that was stopping her, Garrett thought, then the debate was over. "That's okay. I feel 'right' about it enough for both of us."

"Look, you're a busy person and I've taken you away from your responsibilities enough as it is. You can't carry me around all the time and I don't think a wheelchair is going to be able to make it around on that terrain very well—even if I *did* have one," she qualified, "which I don't."

"Like I said, we'll figure it out." And he was already thinking of ways for her to get around that wouldn't involve his carrying her from place to place—even though that idea really didn't bother him in the slightest.

As Garrett had predicted, his brother was nothing but sympathetic and kind to her, not just when they first arrived back at the ranch, but later that afternoon, as well.

She was surprised when Jackson suggested that she stay at the ranch to work on the remainder of her article rather than go through any involved maneuvers to go back and forth between the ranch and the hotel.

"The ranch was built for people," he told her when she began to protest.

Reluctantly—only because she felt as if she was putting the brothers out—she agreed to stay. But when she offered to pay for her room, quoting the same rate that she was currently paying at the hotel, Jackson had cut her off—not with any combination of words, but with one penetrating look. A look that rendered her speechless.

Garrett leaned in toward her. "Didn't know Jackson could be fierce, did you?" he asked in what wouldn't have passed for a whisper in any culture.

She looked at Jackson rather than at Garrett. "I had my suspicions," she said.

With Jackson on board regarding the new temporary housing arrangements, Garrett immediately volunteered to drive back into town to check her out of the hotel and bring her things back to the ranch.

Again she felt uncomfortable being accommodated this way.

"I should go with you," Kim protested.

"Why?" Garrett asked. "I know how to pack and you can't possibly have anything at the hotel that I haven't seen before."

"It's not that," she told him impatiently. "I just can't have you doing all this for me."

Her protest mystified him. He'd been taught that helping one another was a good thing and had abided by that rule for most of his life.

"Why?" he asked.

"Because it's just not right," she insisted.

"I'm not complaining. Why should you?" Garrett asked.

Kim sighed. "Why are you being so nice?" she asked.

"Did it ever occur to you that maybe I just *am* nice?" he asked her, an amused smile playing on his lips as he looked at her.

Kim felt something stirring inside her again, just as

she had on several other occasions when he had looked at her like that. Just as she had—in spades—when she suddenly found herself flat on the ground with Garrett's body pressing down against hers.

"Yes," she answered quietly, "it did."

The room suddenly turned warm around him. Very, very warm. Had Rosa not been a few steps away, getting an early start on dinner in the kitchen, not to mention that, judging by the noise being generated, there was someone else in the room next to them, he would have given in to the very strong temptation and kissed her.

But that would have only complicated a situation that was already complicated enough. So he took a step back instead and said, "I'll be back before you know it."

Sitting on the sofa, she shifted restlessly. "I still don't feel right about this," she told him, a fine edge in her voice.

About to walk away, Garrett stopped then and searched for some sort of a compromise to offer her. Maybe it was about the clothes. Maybe she didn't want him touching any of the intimate things she wore against her skin.

"Would you feel better if I had Debi come with me?" he asked.

Debi, as far as she knew, was still working at the clinic and would be until well after six. She had been impressed and in awe of the hours that Debi, Holly, the other nurse and the two physicians put in at the clinic. At one point or another, they were seeing and treating virtually the entire town, the outlying area, as well as the reservation, which she'd learned had no medical office on the premises whatsoever. She'd already made up her mind to suggest another article on them to Stan.

Or maybe even a series of articles on the small town, she now thought. The idea of a potential series excited her.

But right now, she had a more immediate issue to face.

"I'd feel better if you took me," she said.

Garrett thought for a moment, weighing the pros and cons of taking her with him after all, even though in his heart, he felt this was a mistake. He should have just kept walking out the door the way he had started to. It was just a matter of common sense. The sooner he left, the sooner he'd be back.

But he also knew about pride, having not just his own, but having witnessed Jackson coming to terms with it—both the good and the bad. He'd seen it all firsthand and the lessons had stuck with him.

You never strip a person of their pride, or render it inconsequential.

Exhaling an exasperated breath, he crossed back to Kim and scooped her up in his arms. "Anybody ever tell you that you are one damn stubborn woman?"

Kim grinned. She'd won, so she could afford to be magnanimous. "I think you might have mentioned something about that earlier."

"Not nearly strongly enough," Garrett bit off as he began to head for the front door with her.

"Dinner is at seven," Rosa called after him. "Try not to be late. You know how Mr. Jackson feels about you being late."

"I'm well aware of it, Rosa," he called back just before using his elbow to leverage the doorknob and open it.

"You're very talented," Kim observed, watching him. "And patient."

Garrett laughed shortly. "You don't know the half of it."

She probably didn't, Kim thought. He came across as cool and laid-back, but inside his head, the wheels were always turning. Not conniving, just turning—which was the basic difference between a bad guy and a good one. And Garrett was very obviously one of the good guys.

"Thank you," she told him.

He took her words to mean that she was thanking him for giving in to her and letting her come along. As if he'd really had a choice.

"Yeah, sure."

When he felt her tighten her arms around his neck in a brief, heartfelt hug, he decided that it was in his best interest not to say anything more but just keep walking. Because if he said something, it would lead to something else, which in turn just might make him turn around, take her back inside to her new room and act on what he was feeling.

He had a feeling she wouldn't push him away.

Keeping quiet and walking was the most sensible, if not the most rewarding, way to go.

Chapter Fourteen

On the way back to the hotel, Garrett tried one last time to talk Kim into remaining in the truck, although he knew before he started how this would go.

And he was right.

"Not that I don't enjoy riding around in your truck with you, but I didn't come all this way just to sit in the truck while you go upstairs and pack up my things," she told him.

"So that's a no," he concluded.

"Definitely a no. And don't even think about walking away and leaving me here because I'll find a way to come hobbling after you," she warned.

He laughed shortly as he rounded the hood of his vehicle and came around to her side. "I wouldn't put it past you," Garrett said, picking her up out of the cab. "Let's get to it."

Kim slipped her arms around his neck and smiled triumphantly. "Let's."

Garrett ignored the rather knowing stare he garnered from the young woman behind the reception desk and headed straight for the elevator with Kim. He didn't think that Kim noticed the way the hotel employee was eyeing them until she said, "That receptionist thinks

I've had a few too many and that you're taking me up to my room to have your way with me."

"Then she'll be disappointed when she sees us coming back soon," he concluded.

"Yes," Kim agreed quietly. "*She* will be."

He looked at her then, wondering if it was just his imagination, or if her tone had shifted for a moment. Most likely that was just his own wishful thinking getting the better of him.

The elevator doors opened on her floor and he carried Kim down the hall. Getting the door to the hotel room open from that position—Kim had the key card—seemed tricky to him, but to Garrett's surprise, she managed rather well.

Shouldering the door opened once Kim had unlocked it, he walked into the room and headed straight for her bed. "Okay, I'm going to put you down on the bed," he said needlessly just as he proceeded to do so.

"Thanks for the heads-up," she teased, then grew serious as the situation sank in. "I can't reach anything from here," she protested.

"Exactly." The single word echoed with finality. "I'm going to be the one emptying out your closet and the bureau drawers."

"What do I get to do?" She hated sitting on the sidelines, even when it came to something as inconsequential as this.

"You get to supervise," he told her. "I've got a feeling that you're really good at supervising and telling people what to do," he added with an amused smile.

She pretended to narrow her eyes and level a pointed stare at him. "Was that a dig?"

"An observation," he corrected. "Remember, Lady

Doc said she wanted you to stay off your feet for twenty-four hours."

"She said foot, not feet," Kim pointed out, even though she remained where she was—at least for the time being.

He crossed to the bureau that was on the opposite wall. "Unless you were really, really good at playing hopscotch as a kid, I don't recommend hopping around on one foot right now."

There had been no actual children's games in her childhood. The emphasis, right from the start, had always been on learning. Playing was reserved for those who had no desire to get ahead, or so her parents had maintained.

"Hop-what?"

He'd just assumed that video games had been her games of choice and responded now by flashing her another quick grin.

"I rest my case," he said, pulling open the bureau's top drawer. After scooping up some of the drawer's contents into his hands, he brought the items over to the bed and deposited them next to her in a heap. "I thought maybe you'd want to fold them before you put them into your suitcase."

Not waiting for an answer, he went to the closet and opened it, assuming that the suitcase he'd just mentioned was on the closet floor. When neither one of the two suitcases he'd help her with turned out to be there, he turned around and looked at Kim quizzically.

She knew exactly what he was about to ask. "They're under the bed."

Crossing back to her bed, Garrett knelt down not far

from where she was sitting and felt around underneath. He didn't have to search very far.

"Why would you put them there?" Garrett asked as he pulled out first one, then the other suitcase from beneath the bed.

She answered without any hesitation. "So I had them within reach if I suddenly had to take off in the middle of the night."

Rising, he placed the first suitcase on the bed, then popped open its locks. It was still partially packed. That in itself seemed odd to him.

"Why would you have to suddenly take off?" he asked.

She felt just a little foolish now and thought of just shrugging away his question. But she'd come this far; to pretend to *not* have a reason for her action was even worse in her estimation than giving the reason she *did* have.

"California training," she told him. When his quizzical expression remained, she elaborated. "My family and I lived through one big earthquake in San Francisco. My parents made a huge point of always being prepared. They *insisted* on it. Having a packed suitcase within reach when you were asleep was part of that."

"Seems like an unsettling way to live." He knew he couldn't do it. "You could always move," he suggested, bringing the rest of the clothes from the bureau over to the bed.

Kim shrugged. "I never really thought about it. San Francisco is home base," she told him. "Besides," she continued with a trace of defensiveness, "every place has some kind of 'inconvenience' or natural disaster going against it. Texas has tornadoes and floods," she pointed out.

"Can't argue that," he replied.

The truth was he didn't want to argue about anything with her. This injury of hers meant that she was probably going to stay around a little longer than she had originally planned, but he knew that a few extra days didn't change anything. Kim would still be leaving soon. He wanted to make the most of the time that he had left. Having her on the ranch would certainly cut into the downtime of her traveling to and from town and he liked that.

But he found himself wanting more.

Garrett tried to tell himself that it was human nature to want more, but somehow that didn't quite seem to square things for him. He was always about just rolling with the punches, about coming to terms with the various changes that life brought.

But this one—watching Kim leave—would be really rough on him and that disturbed him more than he was happy about.

"Seems like an awful lot of stuff to pack for such a short stay," he commented, bringing over a second armload from the closet. He was drawing out the process, not wanting to wrinkle any of the clothes he was bringing to her. He was also enjoying their "alone time" here in the hotel room for as long as he could. "Is it part of your 'be prepared' mantra?" he asked.

"One and the same," she told him, adding with a grin, "You're catching on."

"Doesn't exactly take a rocket scientist," he countered. If he hadn't seen the connection, it would have pretty much meant that he was an idiot in his opinion.

Was that the yardstick he used to measure himself against? Kim wondered. Something that would have only been achieved thanks to at least two college degrees? Was Garrett just being modest, or was it that he didn't see himself on the same level as she was?

"Don't have to be a rocket scientist to be bright," she told him.

He paused in midstep, surprised. "Was *that* a compliment?" he asked.

"More like an observation," she replied, echoing the words he had used just a few minutes ago.

"You know," Garrett continued, abruptly changing the subject as he went back to collect more things from the closet, "with you staying on a few more days, you'll be here for the Christmas-tree ceremony."

This was a tiny dot of a town. The idea of any kind of official ceremony seemed almost incongruous to her. "You have a Christmas-tree ceremony in Forever?" she questioned.

"Every year. Miss Joan gets together a team from town and sends them into the woods. They pick out the biggest good-looking tree they can find to bring back on the flat-bed truck she rents for the occasion. Then everyone gets a chance to hang some of the decorations on it. Kind of brings everybody closer together. It's a nice tradition this time of year. Normally, she does it earlier in the month, but things kind of got away from her this year."

"If it's such a big deal, why didn't someone take over for her?" Kim asked, thinking that to be the logical solution.

He laughed. "Because nobody usurps Miss Joan.

Trust me, it's less complicated just waiting for her to get to it. Part of the tradition," he further explained.

Everyone joining in for a mutual goal around the holidays. That seemed impossibly sweet.

"Sounds nice," she had to admit. She wasn't aware that her tone sounded wistful.

But Garrett was.

"Your family have any kind of traditions it follows for the holidays?" he asked.

Unlike his, her laugh was dry and without any humor. "Other than who could get invited to the splashiest party of the season?" It was a rhetorical question she didn't expect him to comment on. "No. They're not very big on Christmas, or any holiday for that matter. Everyone kind of goes their own way." And they had been for a long time now, she thought sadly.

"How about when you were a kid?" he asked. He could feel his sympathy being aroused. He knew she didn't want any, but at this point it was hard keeping it contained.

She lifted her shoulders and let them drop again. "Same thing, really. My parents were too busy attending social events that promised to advance their positions and careers. My sisters did things with their friends, or people they *said* were their friends."

He was only interested in how all this affected her. "And you?"

She turned her face away from him. "I really don't want to talk about it."

"You are definitely coming to the Christmas-tree ceremony with me. If that wasn't a factor," he told her, indicating her bandaged ankle, "I'd ask Miss Joan to include you in the tree selection process."

But there was no way she could hobble around through the woods in that condition and he knew she wouldn't allow him to carry her.

Why was he saying that to her? "The ceremony's for the people of the town, right?" she asked, already knowing the answer.

"Right."

Garrett still didn't look as if he understood, she thought, so she spelled it out for him. "Well, I don't belong."

"Anyone in or around Forever this time of year 'belongs,'" he informed her, then went on to say, "Might as well give up. You're not wiggling out of this."

"I thought I was supposed to be the bossy one," she reminded him.

"It's catching," he shot back—then laughed. "Sorry, but I'm bigger than you are. That means that you're coming."

He reached for the last pile of intimate apparel she had put together, intending on placing it in the suitcase that was open on the floor near the bed. The pile was just to the left of her and close to the end of the bed. As he reached over to get it, he had to bend forward and almost over her.

With less than an inch between them, he brushed against her. He started to apologize—but never got the chance to actually say the words.

Taking the collar of his jacket in her hands, Kim suddenly pulled him into her just enough to seal her mouth to his.

The apology he was about to say never materialized. Instead, something else came in its place. A feeling that was completely unexpected, hot and fiery, and fundamentally pleasing on far too many levels even to begin to count.

The clothes and packing temporarily abandoned, Garrett closed his arms around her and pulled Kim to him, his mouth never leaving hers.

He deepened the kiss that had ambushed him, savoring every incremental moment.

Wishing it could go on forever.

Wishing that he could allow it to flower into something more.

But that would be taking advantage of not just the situation, but of her, as well, and as much as he found himself responding to her, as much as he *wanted* her, he knew he couldn't, in all good conscience, allow himself to continue it. To take this to the next level the way every single fiber of his body was literally *begging* him to.

Attempting to summon strength he wasn't entirely certain he possessed, Garrett drew his head back. At the same time, he took hold of her shoulders to make sure that the space he created stayed there between them.

The way he felt at this moment, he wasn't really sure how long he could make himself stay back. His desire for her was already beginning to wear away his resolve.

"If that's how you react to being invited to the ceremony, I can't wait to see what you're like *after* the ceremony." He was attempting to joke around with her, but the words themselves gave him away. They came out sounding so breathless that it took considerable effort to form the words and get them out without gasping between each one.

She looked at him, stunned and hurt that he was rejecting her like this.

But the expression in his eyes told her he wasn't rejecting her, he was trying to protect her.

The hell with that.

She didn't need to be protected from him, although, she thought in dark amusement, he might need to be protected from her.

"Don't make me beg, Garrett. I can't get up on my knees," she told him. And then, as if to contradict herself, she attempted to do just that. It didn't go well, but she learned something. "At least, not on both of them."

"We can't do this," he insisted, trying to appeal to her common sense.

"Why?" This was new to her. She'd never had to try to convince someone to make love with her before. Usually, if anything, she had to find a way to turn them down. "Don't you want me?"

He knew that if he told her that he didn't, then she would back away, taking temptation with her. But if he told her that, she'd be hurt and he didn't want to hurt her. And besides, it would be a lie and he didn't want to lie. Not to her.

"So much that it literally hurts," he confessed.

"Then what's wrong?" she asked, really confused.

"It's your foot," he told her.

"Unless there's something really kinky in your plans, feet don't come directly into play in lovemaking."

"No, you're supposed to be resting it," he reminded her, even as he felt himself losing the struggle not by inches, but by yards.

"It'll be on the bed the entire time," she promised, her eyes shining in anticipation. "Can't ask to rest it more than that."

He could literally feel himself burning for her. He

couldn't remember the last time something had been this difficult for him.

"Damn it, I can't say no to you."

"Then don't," she whispered, reaching up to touch his face. She drew it—and his mouth—down to hers. "Don't," she repeated seductively.

The struggle with himself, such as it was, was over in less than a heartbeat. Garrett found he couldn't fight his own desires—and her—at the same time. Any resolve he had to keep away from her for her own good crumbled and blew away on the wind, every trace vanishing as if it had never existed.

His heart pounding, Garrett ached to hold her, to have her.

But even so, he had to give her one last chance to tell him no. He wanted Kim to know that if she did have a change of heart, all she had to do was tell him. Hard as it was, he'd understand.

He framed her face with his hands, looking deep into her eyes. "Are you absolutely sure you won't regret this?"

"What I am absolutely sure of," she said as she balanced herself on her good knee and pulled the sleeves of his jacket down off his arms, "is that you'll be the one with regrets if you try to walk away now."

Garrett was quick to shrug the jacket off the rest of the way, letting it fall to the floor.

His eyes only on hers, he knelt on the bed and before opening so much as a single button on her blouse, he began kissing her over and over again. He was heating her body, as well as her soul and somehow, he was making her want him even more than she had just a minute ago.

Until this very moment, she wouldn't have thought that was possible.

It was going to happen, her body sang as she surrendered herself to the transformation.

It's going to happen.

The feeling only heightened as she felt his lips trailing along her neck, going down beneath her chin and then to the hint of the swell of her breasts.

Her body shuddered, waiting for fulfillment.

Longing for it.

Kim felt as if she was standing at the gates of ecstasy, and she was more than willing and eager to push those gates open and enter.

Chapter Fifteen

He just kept surprising her.

The few men that she had known to this degree of intimacy had all been adequate lovers; a couple had even been above adequate. But lovemaking with any of them had not lasted very long. Foreplay—if there was any—was over in one, sometimes two, blinks of an eye. The effects of the entire experience didn't linger for long—and neither did they.

The best summation of even the best of those experiences was that it was intense—and brief. All parties involved moved on very quickly.

She discovered that Garrett did not subscribe to any part of that philosophy.

Lovemaking with the man she thought of affectionately as "the cowboy" was almost lyrical by comparison. It was, first off, drawn out and beautiful, with one moment flowering into the next, building on what came before, preparing for what was to come next.

Anticipation clawed at her almost from the very first moment.

She tugged away the rest of Garrett's clothing, desperate to run the palms of her hands along his tanned, smooth, bare skin.

The instant that she did, Kim could feel heat licking at her very core, urging her on. She sealed her mouth to his, pressed her own naked body—Garrett had been busy while she had been undressing him—against his. She felt his desire growing against her and that immediately served to heighten and intensify her own.

Heighten it to the point that she could barely contain herself.

Any second now he'd come to her, take her, seal their bodies together, and then the sparklers and rockets would go off, showering over them both.

As much as she wanted it, she didn't want this part to end so quickly.

She got her wish.

Garrett held back from indulging in the final union. Instead, he made love to her slowly, with feeling. He made love to every inch of her, stoking the flames with his hands, his lips, his tongue, causing eruption after eruption to go off within her body.

Her desire for him all but overwhelmed her.

HE LIKED IMMERSING himself in the sound and feel of her. Twisting and turning beneath his touch, his lips and tongue, she'd anointed him with her sweat, claimed him with her questing touch that traveled over the length of him and all but brought him to the brink himself by just the power of her lips alone.

He wanted her.

Wanted her so badly that he virtually *ached*.

Had there only been himself to consider, he would have taken Kim the moment he had gone one step inside of the hotel room.

But he wanted her to enjoy what was happening—to

remember what was happening. He wanted, when time and space had come between them, for her to pause and relive this, thinking of him fondly—and maybe with a little bit of longing, as well.

He wanted her to feel what he knew in his gut he would feel, no matter how many years would come to separate them.

But he had reached his limit and as much as he wanted to play this out a little longer for her sake, he couldn't.

It was time.

Rolling onto her, bringing his body up so that their eyes met and their torso blended, he laced his fingers through hers. And even at this last moment, this final moment before fulfillment, Kim was *still* his first concern.

"Are you all right?" he whispered, his eyes never leaving hers.

She almost laughed then, the situation seemed so impossibly sweet—so *Garrett*, she realized—but she managed to stifle the sound.

"So all right," she told him hoarsely, "they haven't even invented a word for it yet."

Unlike her, Garrett laughed at her comment. Laughed as if he was sharing the same sentiment with her.

The sound echoed within her chest as she never took her eyes off his. She melted without any resistance right then and there.

Kissing her, Garrett thrust himself into her as gently as possible. He felt her catching her breath, the gasp muffled against his mouth. When he stiffened, then tried to draw back, to allow her to either gather herself together or change her mind at this late juncture, Kim wove her arms around his neck and held him to her, the message clear. He wasn't to go anywhere.

She felt his mouth curving against hers as he remained.

And then the dance began, growing more and more impassioned, moving more and more quickly. It was as if they were urging one another on, lifting each other up. One could not climb up without the other.

Joined as one, they reached the highest pinnacle that they could aspire to and reached it in a frenzy—the next moment, a shower of stars encompassed them, making everything almost ten times as intense.

She held on to him as if something within her feared she'd fall off the edge of the world if she didn't.

Euphoria wrapped tightly around them, sealing in the ecstatic feeling of well-being. But eventually, no matter how tightly the seal, it allowed air and reality to come in and break apart the dream.

She wanted to lie there a little while longer, savoring what had happened, memorizing it from every possible angle before it began to fade from her mind. But the very last thing in the world she wanted was to have Garrett think of her as being needy, so instead of lingering and enjoying the stellar moment until it faded into nothingness, she deliberately took the lead and pulled into herself.

She could feel his confusion. Could feel her own need for him threatening to overwhelm her for a second time. Forcing herself to turn into him, she said as casually as possible, "I think Rosa said something about being on time for dinner."

On time? Right, he silently jeered.

"I'm afraid that bronco has probably long since burst out of his rodeo pen," Garrett speculated, wondering how she could be thinking about something so mundane as dinner and curfews when all he wanted to do was lie here, holding her against him, feeling her heart beat in rhythm with his own.

It seemed like such a small thing.

But it was everything.

Kim angled the small wristwatch she was wearing so that she could make out the time. "No, I think if we hurry, we can make it back just in time—or at least no more than fifteen minutes late."

Every bone in his body was exhausted from love-making. There was no way he could get dressed and bolt out of here like an Olympian in training. If she thought she could—and on a bandaged ankle yet—she was in a hell of a lot better shape than he was.

"I don't think I know how to hurry right now."

And then Garrett raised himself up on his elbow, eyeing her more closely. Was he missing something? He had enjoyed making love with her more than he could recall ever enjoying being with any other woman. Had it just been one-sided on his part?

"Are you trying to tell me you want to make a break for it and get back to somewhere—*anywhere*—just so that you don't have to be alone with me?" he asked her bluntly.

Dear God, where had he gotten that idea? She was just trying to keep him safe and away from a reprimand. "What I'm telling you is that I don't want Jackson to have something else to hold against me."

He grinned, laughter entering his eyes. "The only thing that is going to be held against you this afternoon is me."

Then, to make good on his promise, Garrett pulled her to him one last time and kissed her. Kissed her so soundly that he all but branded her.

And then he drew back. "Okay. Now I guess we'd better get dressed and head back to the ranch."

He eyed Kim as she sat up, wearing nothing but a wistful smile and he could feel the pull of desire building all over again.

"Need any help getting dressed?" he offered.

She glanced at Garrett as she slid to the edge of the bed and reached for her things. "I've got a feeling that if I took you up on that offer, we'd never leave the room."

Garrett appeared almost solemn as he shook his head while he gathered together his cast-off clothing. "Beautiful *and* smart. That's one hell of a lethal combination," he commented.

She was about to ask him what he meant by "lethal," but then stopped herself just in time—for a very good reason. She had a strong feeling that he'd demonstrate rather than tell her, and that would just be asking for trouble.

Trouble had never looked so terribly virile and attractive, she couldn't help thinking as she hurried into her clothes. For two cents, she'd be more than willing to invite trouble back into her waiting arms.

Later, there might be time for this later, she silently promised herself. As for now, there were hoops to jump through and she still had an article to finish. That meant continuing to stay on her older host's good side. She already had learned that accomplishing that little feat involved not opposing the man unless it was very, very necessary.

"I WAS JUST going to send out Bella and Bobbie to find you two," Jackson said as Garrett walked into the dining room, carrying Kim in his arms.

Kim looked at her human chariot quizzically. "Bella and Bobby?"

"Bella and Bobbie are the tracking hounds," he explained, slipping her onto the empty chair positioned next to his. "We use them to track down any runaway horses." And then he turned his head momentarily toward Jackson, although he did avoid looking into his brother's eyes. "Took longer to pack than I thought it would," Garrett told him.

"Uh-huh." It was obvious that the older White Eagle wasn't buying the excuse, but he didn't push it any further—at least not for now.

The next moment, even if he were going to say something else, he would have had to raise his voice or risk being drowned out. As a volley of questions suddenly erupted, coming from not one or two but from all of the teens at the table. And all centering on Kim.

They were asking about her foot, expressing concern about her nerve-shaking encounter with the willful horse, and giving advice on how to avoid what had happened this morning should there ever be a "next time."

Kim tried her best to field the questions. Not all that long ago, she would have viewed these questions as nothing short of an invasion of her privacy. But now she knew better. It was an expression of concern. Concern coming from a group of teens she hadn't even known existed just a little while ago—teens who hadn't known *she* existed a little while ago, as well.

But now they knew and they cared. It seemed almost mind-boggling to her. As mind-boggling as discovering that there was a whole new level of lovemaking she hadn't realized existed.

For now, she focused on the other faces around the table, not Garrett's.

She almost came close to asking one of them why he cared, but that would have ruined the moment and would have been, admittedly, crass and crude.

It occurred to her that she couldn't recall either one of her parents ever really expressing any sort of concern regarding her welfare or the welfare of either one of her sisters.

Neither parent had expressed personal concern at any rate. Their concern only extended to the realm of family pride. She and her sisters were forbidden to do anything that would bring any sort of dishonor to their family, more specifically to her mother and father.

Beyond that, they were free to do whatever they wanted, although they were encouraged—and in a way, rather browbeaten—to do something that would bring more honor to the family.

Her sisters eventually did; she did not. Hence she was the black sheep of the family and would remain so until she finally followed the true path—whatever that was, she thought cynically.

These teens—and this man who sat beside her—behaved more like family than her own family did.

That begged for further exploration.

Maybe, she thought, slanting a glance in Garrett's direction, this accident was a good thing. It gave her an excuse to linger here on the ranch—and near Forever—a little while longer. It also gave her the excuse to take part in that tree ceremony thing that Garrett had mentioned.

She found herself looking forward to it in much the same way a child looked forward to the actual whole

Christmas experience. Looking forward to it even as she tried to tell herself that she was being childish. She had been taught that Christmas was strictly a retail thing to allow stores one last financial boost before the end of the year.

She might be telling herself that, but she really wasn't listening. Because Garrett had managed, with only a few well-placed words, to make it all sound exciting.

"Kim and I are going into town tomorrow afternoon," Garrett told his brother. "This year's team will probably be back in town with the tree by then," Garrett speculated, further explaining his reason for going in.

A couple of questions from the occupants of the dining room table told Kim that the teens knew less about the town's Christmas tradition than she did and she found herself jumping in to field and answer the questions that she could.

"Who picks the team?" one tall, gangly teen named Rick who, she had learned, arrived at the ranch two months ago with a chip on his shoulder twice as big as he was, asked.

The fact that she knew the answer to that one ramped up her confidence level. "Miss Joan," she told Rick.

Robert, the shortest teen at the table, asked. "Can anyone get on this 'team'?" She looked to Garrett for input.

He gladly obliged. "Miss Joan's probably got this year's volunteers all set, but maybe if we go really early, Jackson here could put in a good word for you."

"Me? Why me?" Jackson asked, finding himself unexpectedly the center of this conversation.

Garrett's answer was preceded with an amused

chuckle. *As if Jackson doesn't know.* "Because you're the one who reminds her of Sam, not me."

The last explanation brought another round of questions pouring out of the boys, but eventually, the questions were answered, the situation settled. And it was abundantly clear that because of the tree decorating, no one was going to be working on the ranch tomorrow. They were all looking forward to taking part, as best they could, in this unifying celebration.

For some of the teens, this meant getting back to caring about things like family and holidays; for others it was a totally new experience, one that held enormous appeal.

"Well, it looks like I've got a rebellion on my hands," Jackson commented, looking around the table at the boys. "Guess I might as well go along with it or risk getting trampled for getting in the way." And then he spared Kim a long glance. "No offense intended, Kim," Jackson told her.

But Kim was nothing if not resilient. That much, she felt she *could* thank her parents for.

"None taken," she assured him. She looked around the table herself. The teens were all smiling, all anticipating the following day. With only a well-turned phrase and just by dropping a hint or two, no promises, just possibilities, Jackson and Garrett had managed to give the boys—some of whom, she knew by the research she'd done the other day, had been well on their way to becoming hardened criminals—something to look forward to. Something, she was willing to bet, they might have turned their backs on not all that long ago.

They had a gift, Garrett and Jackson, she couldn't help thinking. A gift for reaching unreachable boys.

Stan, her editor, had been right: there was a very good story here—and he had given it to her. Not so that she would produce a fluff piece, but so that the article would help turn her into a better, sharper writer who could see beneath the cosmetics down to the actual heart of the story.

She realized that now.

I won't let you down, Stan, she silently promised. *I won't let you down.*

Chapter Sixteen

"I can't believe you got Miss Joan to say yes," Kim marveled the next day.

It was close to two in the afternoon, and she and Garrett were sitting on a bench outside of Forever's general store, sharing a rather large container of coffee that Garrett had picked up for them at the diner.

Kim was referring to the fact that all of the teens who were currently staying at the Healing Ranch had gotten to go with the officially selected team who were searching for the town's Christmas tree.

"Miss Joan does *not* strike me as a lady who changes her mind once it's made up," Kim told him, "and from what you said, she'd already sent in her 'tree finding' team really early this morning."

"She's not and she did," Garrett replied, enjoying just sitting out here with Kim like this, watching the winter sun highlighting her hair, turning it into a warm shade of black.

So warm that his fingertips itched to touch it to see if it felt as silky now as it had yesterday.

Kim looked at him, confused by his answer. "If that's the case, why did she let those teens go? I mean, they're not in town," she pointed out, gesturing around the area, "and unless she's got them tied up in some cellar, they're off in your brother's truck, riding around with everyone else and looking for that so-called 'perfect' tree she told them to 'fetch.'"

"They're not tied up in some cellar," Garrett assured her, laughing. "I told you, Miss Joan's got a soft spot in her heart when it comes to Jackson. That makes it hard for her to say no to him if he really asks her for something—which, given that he's Jackson, he very rarely does." So saying, Garrett leaned back for a moment, studying the woman beside him.

She could feel his eyes on her and it both made her want to preen and shift uncomfortably. Was he scrutinizing her and finding her lacking? She talked a good game, but when she came right down to it, beneath the verbal bravado, she had no real self-confidence.

Another bonus from growing up in the household that she did.

"What?" she finally asked Garrett when he continued looking at her in silence.

His smile was slow, unfurling a little at a time and drawing her in before she knew what was happening. "I was just thinking about how surprised I was to see how good you looked on Annabel this morning."

No one could have been more surprised than she. Out of the blue, in the middle of all her questions about the way he and his brother operated the ranch, Garrett had watched her oddly, then asked if she would be willing to come to the stables with him and look at one of the horses.

Since the whole operation of the ranch and what it did for the teens who came was hinged on the horses, she couldn't see how she could turn him down. But in order to reach the horse, she would have to rely on Garrett carrying her over to the stables and then inside.

She was beginning to hate being immobilized this way. If anything, her right shoulder felt even worse than it had when she'd initially attempted to use the crutches the doctor had given her. And although she loved the feel of Garrett's arms around her and having him carrying her around, there was no getting away from the fact that she felt like a huge burden. She was definitely *not* accustomed to not being able to pull her own weight.

She'd sat on a bale of hay within the stall as he introduced her to the mare he'd wanted her to see. He'd then gone to explain—at length—the different parts of the saddle and harness and their functions as he saddled up the horse.

The last thing she had expected him to do, once Annabel was saddled, was to lift her up and into the saddle.

"I don't know how to ride a horse," she'd protested, not at all sure what he was trying to do.

"Not much to it," he'd answered. "The horse does most of the work. All you have to do is sit there and look pretty—and you've already got that part down pat," he assured her. And then he'd placed the reins in her hands. "It'll make Annabel think you're steering her."

Once he'd seen that she was holding the reins in her hand without appearing ready to strangle the mare, he'd taken hold of the mare's bit and led her slowly out into the corral.

None of the boys—they were all in town by then—were there to see her and gradually, bit by bit, the agitation Kim was experiencing began to recede. Especially since Garrett was slowly feeding her instructions.

She stopped being afraid that she would suddenly go

flying right over the horse's head and began to take in the world that was around her.

She discovered that there was a lot to see from this vantage point.

Looking at Garrett now as they sat before the general store, she realized that she was still "riding high" on the empowering enthusiasm he had managed to generate with that simple act of getting her to mount the mare.

"Maybe when we get back, we can go off for a ride together," she suggested hopefully.

The comment came out of the blue and took a second for him to process. "It'll probably be dark by then," was his guess.

She wasn't about to give up that easily. "Tomorrow, then?"

"Sure, tomorrow's a possibility," Garrett agreed, then qualified his answer. "As long as you remember that you have to be able to walk before you can run—and that includes galloping."

Kim's mouth dropped open. It was as if Garrett could read her mind. The exhilaration of seeing the world while she was perched high on her horse made her want to experience feeling the wind whipping through her hair—which it would if the horse she was on broke into a gallop. But she definitely hadn't said as much to Garrett.

Apparently she didn't have to, she concluded.

"How did you know?" she couldn't help asking him now.

He grinned broadly. "Because while you've been studying us at the ranch, I've been studying you." *Quite a bit, actually*, he added silently. *And I like what I've come to know.* "I saw that look in your eyes when you realized that you weren't going to go flying off Annabel unless you did something to really set her off or spook her."

It was funny, but she knew the exact moment he was referring to. That was the moment she'd felt almost invincible.

"You have no idea how liberating it felt to be able to move around without waiting to be carried from place to place."

The smile he was attempting to keep back struggled to the surface as he said, "Technically, Annabel was carrying you."

But she shook her head. "Not the same thing," Kim disagreed. She expected him to offer a rebuttal. He didn't.

Instead, he agreed with her, endearing himself to her just a little more. "Changes your perspective on things, doesn't it?"

"Sitting on top of Annabel?" She could feel her smile reaching her eyes as she said, "Yes, it does."

He wanted her to realize that the effects she was experiencing went deeper than she'd first thought. "Not just the fact that you can move around more freely on the mare, but just working with her in general. That's what Jackson discovered when Sam gave him the responsibility of caring for his horse—and that's what we do now with the teenagers we work with.

"The horses are the key we use to unlock the decent kid trapped inside the swaggering, the boasting, the budding would-be criminal. So far," and he was rather proud of this, "it's been working pretty well."

"I can see that."

It wasn't hard to see how much the ranch and what

they were accomplishing meant to Garrett, as well as to Jackson. She wanted to help assure them that the situation wasn't going to change—especially not because of something as cold and crass as money.

The wheels in her head hadn't stopped turning since she and Garrett had started talking about the ranch. "You mentioned that the ranch has money problems—this could be the way out."

She was talking fast and he wasn't sure he understood where she was going with this. "Slow down," he urged. "*What* could be the way out?"

Taking a breath, she tried again. "The article I'm writing could bring the kind of attention you and Jackson need to get people interested in the Healing Ranch."

That had been the argument he'd used to try to convince Jackson to agree to the interview to begin with. She didn't have to sell him on that.

"To send more kids here," Garrett agreed, assuming that was what she was getting at.

"No, to invest in."

His brow furrowed. "I don't follow."

She spelled it out for him, trying to keep her voice from growing louder and faster as she explained the vision she had for the ranch.

"Jackson could sell franchises to the name, have other people set up ranches just like this one—kind of like fast-food chains do with franchises. You and Jackson could stand to make a great deal of money, not to mention that you'd be able to keep this main branch of the Healing Ranch open and running—at a profit instead of a deficit."

"You're talking about turning this into a business."

It wasn't a question but a statement. His expression remained unchanged.

She'd expected him to get as excited about this idea as she had and she felt somewhat disappointed that he wasn't. "Well, yes."

Garrett shook his head. He knew how Jackson felt about things better than anyone. His brother would never go for this.

"Jackson's not interested in making money, or selling off franchises. He's interested in helping troubled boys who think they have no options open to them except to throw their lot in with the local gang. Kids aren't hamburgers, Kim."

Then, because Kim looked so disheartened and frustrated, he leaned over and kissed her cheek. He did it quickly, not wanting to give anyone who might see them—the town had more than its share of eager gossips—something to talk about.

"It won't fly with him, but it was a very nice thought. Thanks for trying to help," he told her with sincerity.

Kim, however, was not one to give up easily. "It's more than a nice thought," she protested. "It's the only way—"

Whatever else she was about to say was suddenly drowned out by the excited volley of voices coming from a group of young children. The latter had been keeping vigil, watching for the caravan of trucks to return, following like a parade behind the flatbed truck bearing the town's Christmas tree.

High pitched voices both clashed and blended as cries of: "It's here!"

"The Christmas tree's here!" and "They're back with

the town's tree!" as well as other excited exclamations flew through the air.

Kim realized that Garrett was on his feet, looking every bit as excited as the kids were.

It was catching. Instead of the jaded attitude she had adopted and developed over the years, she found herself responding to this childlike enthusiasm that was all around her. No matter what the age, it was as if everyone in the proximity of the town square had suddenly developed the exuberant enthusiasm of a hyperactive ten-year-old.

She found it amazingly refreshing and somehow life-affirming to become excited about something so simple and down to earth as a Christmas tree.

Garrett bent down to her level for a second. "I'm going to help Miss Joan bring out the decorations," he told her, then added, "I'll be right back. You stay here."

"Well, since I seem to have left my wings at the ranch, I guess I'll have to," Kim said flippantly, trying not to let him see her frustration. She wanted to be right there at his side, rushing off to get the decorations with him, not sitting here like a useless bump on a log.

"Be *right back*," he promised, hurrying off even faster than he normally would have.

"Aren't you going to join in?"

The curious, high-pitched voice came from her left almost as soon as Garrett had disappeared into the crowd.

Kim looked around and discovered a little girl standing less than two feet away from her.

The small blonde girl, roughly eight years old, wearing jeans and a checkered blue flannel shirt, as well as stitched boots, was looking at her curiously. Her small oval face was animated as if she was trying to understand why, when everyone in town was hurrying to meet the incoming truck, this lady stayed sitting on the bench in front of the general store.

"What's your name?" Kim asked her.

"Bekka. With two *k*'s. Momma says that makes it special."

"Well, hello, Bekka with two *k*'s. It's nice to meet you." She smiled at the little girl, extending her hand to her. "I'm Kim."

The little girl solemnly took the hand and shook it. "Aren't you going to join in, Kim?" Bekka asked, repeating her question, personalizing it this time around.

Kim sighed. "I can't."

The small face puckered as Bekka apparently tried to understand. "Don't you like Christmas trees?" she asked with the unabashed directness of a child who hadn't learned to be inhibited yet, or to think before she spoke. "I do," she added.

"Oh, I really like Christmas trees," Kim replied. "But I can't walk." She pointed to the bandage around her ankle and leg.

Bekka squatted down to inspect the bandage more closely. She moved around it slowly. Finished, she rose up to her feet again.

"You could lean on me if you like," she offered. "I won't move fast, so you won't get more hurt if that's what you're worried about."

The generous gesture on the child's part both touched and concerned Kim at the same time. Bekka was decidedly too friendly. Though she hated to think about it, there were people who could take advantage of that.

"Didn't your mother teach you not to talk to strangers?" she asked Bekka.

The little face puckered again, as if trying to reconcile the question with what had already come to pass. "You're not a stranger. I know your name. And, anyway, Momma says that strangers are just friends who don't know it yet."

How hopelessly naive, Kim couldn't help thinking—and yet, how wonderful if people in this town actually believed that and lived accordingly.

Wouldn't it be wonderful if the world was really like that?

But it wasn't and none of the people in this town would probably be able to survive in the kind of city she came from. Still, it was heartening to know that trust like this—the kind that Bekka displayed—did exist in some places in this country.

She smiled at the little girl. "Thank you very much for your offer, but I'm waiting for my friend to come back."

"You mean Garrett." Bekka nodded solemnly, as if she understood the reasoning behind her new friend's words. "Okay. But if you need me, just call me. Remember, my name's Bekka."

Kim grinned and gave in to the impulse to tousle the little girl's hair. "With two *k*'s. Yes. I remember."

The little girl beamed at her. "I gotta go, Kim. Miss Joan's bringing out the decorations!" she exclaimed, excited, and with that she scooted away. Within less than a minute, she'd managed to disappear completely into the crowd.

The mention of the decorations being brought out had Kim scanning the crowd, looking for Garrett.

When she did finally locate him, she felt a funny little flutter in her chest, as well as a tightening in the muscles in her abdomen.

Terrific. You're having conversations with an eight-year-old and behaving like a high school adolescent. You don't get out of this town soon, you're going to regress to a zygote before Stan gets a chance to tell you what's wrong with your article.

Her editor's idea of complimenting her on her work was in only finding five things to complain about in her article instead of more. She was still trying to reconcile herself to his approach.

"See, not long," Garrett said, slightly breathless as he dropped into the seat beside her again. He'd had to practically fight his way back to Kim because the crowd all seemed to be going in the opposite direction. He felt he now knew what salmon felt like when they had to swim upstream.

Kim sat up a little straighter, trying to get a better view of what was going on.

"It looks like everyone in town is crowding into the town square," she observed, raising her voice to be heard above the din.

"That's because they are," he answered. "Saw Bekka Gallagher talking to you."

A fond smile curved her lips as she nodded. "She offered to help me get to the tree so I could join in the decorating."

He turned to look into the crowd for a second, as if to search for the little girl, then turned back to Kim. "Did you tell her that was my job?"

She laughed at the suggestion. Seeing the tree and the way the town was gathered around it, she decided there was no way she would be able to get close to it. And she certainly didn't expect Garrett to bring her there. It would be too much of a hassle.

"No, of course not."

"Well, it is," he told her with finality.

Then, before she could say anything else—and most likely have her words swallowed up by the crowd—Garrett stood up from the bench. The next moment, Kim found herself airborne. Garrett had swept her up into his arms and, despite the thick crowd, begun to make his way to the tree.

"Garrett, stop, you can't do this," she told him.

"Funny, I thought I was," he responded, never missing a step as he continued walking toward the tree and the huge baskets of decorations that were on the ground around it.

Kim closed her eyes as she slipped her arms around his neck and let herself enjoy the journey.

Chapter Seventeen

Miss Joan was waiting for them. The unofficial town matriarch remained silent until Garrett and Kim finally reached her.

With a regal nod of her head, the woman told Kim, "Seeing as how this is your first Christmas here, you get first pick of whatever decorations you want to put on the tree."

Several suggestions from the crowd came at her at once, flying in from all different directions. Rather than put her down so she could balance herself precariously on one foot and attempt to choose, Garrett continued to hold her in his arms. He bent over the first table that contained several opened boxes displaying a variety of the more delicate decorations, from standard to unique, all in an accommodating large size.

The decorations all seemed to flow into one another, but she made a decision as quickly as possible and picked out a depiction of a Western scene, complete with a sheriff and his office, as well as his horse. The horse had a Christmas wreath hanging around its neck.

Holding it up like a trophy, Kim declared, "This one."

Garrett laughed, wondering if she knew how enthusiastic she sounded. "You can hang more than one, you know."

Rather than take Garrett's word for it, she glanced over her shoulder toward Miss Joan for confirmation. The last thing she wanted was to have the woman think of her as being greedy.

Miss Joan nodded her head solemnly. "It's true. I think over the years we've gotten enough ornaments together to decorate two trees. Grab a few more, then give this sinewy cowboy a break and let him rest for a while. Although," she went on, giving Kim a quick once-over, "all told, you probably don't even weigh a whole hundred pounds."

"As a matter of fact, I'm a hundred and three," Kim told her.

Miss Joan's response was to just shake her head. "I'm surprised you haven't blown away in the wind yet. Definitely have to fatten you up, girl," she said in a voice that would have been eaten up by the din and gone unheard had Garrett not been holding her right next to the woman.

"Miss Joan made it sound as if she thought I was going to be around for a while," she said to Garrett later that night after everyone else in the house had gone to bed.

Somehow, although she wasn't entirely certain of the actual logistics that had been involved, Garrett had wound up in her bed and they had gone on to share another exquisite session of physical exploration, culminating in delicious lovemaking.

Now she was lying beside him, catching her breath and trying not to think too much about anything because all roads led to an inevitable "tomorrow," which, although it loomed on the horizon, would not see them greeting it together.

She didn't want to think about that.

But lying here in silence wasn't acceptable to her either. Not when the silence only seemed to grow and feed her fears about the dark, hollow loneliness that was waiting for her.

"Can't really blame her," Garrett commented. With one arm tucked around her, he had the other beneath his head, acting like a pillow. "Most of the people who stay here for a little while wind up staying in town for a lot longer—like the name says," he reminded her with a grin. "Forever."

This was the first time he'd ever mentioned that. "Oh? Like who?" she asked, thinking that maybe he was just pulling her leg.

"Well, let's see." He gathered her to him a little closer, as if he was preparing to begin telling her a long bed-time story. "You've already met my sister-in-law, Debi. She came here when she brought her brother to Jackson in a last-ditch attempt to turn the kid around. Ryan came around—and Debi married Jackson." He paused to allow that to sink in.

"There's Lady Doc, who came here just to get over a cheating fiancé and wound up falling for Brett Murphy." That in turn had wound up being a real boost for the town, he thought, virtually doubling their doctor population. "Speaking of the Murphys, Liam's wife was a music contractor on her way to audition some band. He saved her from a flash flood and she wound up marrying him, as well as starting him off in his music career. Liam had a song in the top-twenty list last year," he informed her. "Then there's Finn's wife, Connie—

she was with the company that built the hotel. She's still here, building a life, as well.

"Now the sheriff's wife, Olivia, was passing through here, looking for her sister and her baby nephew. Found them both and all three are still here. Matter of fact, her sister's married to Dr. Dan—who, by the way, is also not from around here. Olivia's one of our two lawyers and her sister is Miss Joan's accountant. Oh, and how could I forget, there's—"

He sounded as if he was just getting wound up, Kim thought. Maybe *he* should have been a lawyer, as well. "Okay, okay, I give up," she cried, laughing as she held up her hands in surrender.

With a swift, smooth movement, Garrett caught her hands by her wrists, anchoring them down above her head as he rolled over onto her. There was pure wickedness in his eyes.

"Do you, now?" he asked, the corners of his mouth curving invitingly.

Kim could feel her heart suddenly revving up again like a racing engine, eager to get started. He'd misunderstood her—or maybe she had misunderstood him. At any rate, she wasn't about to get into the subject of her staying or not staying in Forever—he hadn't asked and she wasn't going to lose face by volunteering. The way she saw it, if Garrett actually wanted her to stay, he would have to come out and ask her—and then she would need to think. Obviously moving here would mean rethinking a major part of her life.

But he hadn't asked and she wasn't about to bring it up again.

Instead, she found it much easier just to allow nature to take its course by making love with the man. If nothing else, this would make for a beautiful memory and in the end, that might be all she had left.

Memories of a happier time.

Memories of Garrett.

"I MUST SAY, I'm rather surprised. It reads really well, Lee."

Stan's booming voice was coming over loud and clear on her cell phone—which for once was on the receiving end of decent reception. But even so, she still wasn't fully grasping what the usually stony-faced, hard-to-please editor-in-chief was telling her.

She'd worked for him in one capacity or another for as long as she'd been selling freelance articles to the magazines he oversaw and in all that time, he had never been so complimentary before. He had definitely never been even remotely close to effusive about an article she had worked on.

It made her wonder if he was trying to soften the blow that was coming.

"Are you firing me, Stan?" she asked, trying her best not to sound upset.

There was silence on the other end, as if Stan was uncertain how to answer her question. With every nanosecond that went by, her stomach sank down a little farther.

Had she guessed right? *Was* he firing her?

And then Stan finally spoke. "I just said the article reads well. How do you get *fired* out of that?" he asked impatiently.

Maybe he *wasn't* firing her. A wave of relief washed over her. "I thought that maybe you were trying to soften the blow before it landed," she confessed.

She heard him snort dismissively on the other end. "Kid, this is me. Saunders. When have I *ever* softened a blow?" he asked.

She smiled sheepishly even though he wasn't anywhere where he could see it. "Always a first time."

"Yeah, and the next meteor might take a huge chunk out of the earth, but not likely," he bit off. "I'm serious, Lee. This is a good piece. A *really* good piece," he repeated. "I think you're finally becoming a writer, kid. Take a break—or better yet, let that break of yours heal," he instructed, apparently remembering what had stranded her on that ranch outside of Forever for this long. "We'll talk after Christmas."

"After Christmas?" she echoed, stunned. He'd just paid her the ultimate compliment in his world and told her he thought her article was good. She felt as if she was walking twelve feet above the ground. It made her eager to sink her teeth into another assignment, not come to a skidding stop and just ferment. "Don't you have anything on tap now?"

"Yeah, spiked eggnog," he cracked, his voice sounding particularly gravelly as he said it. "Go get yourself some, too. Or maybe even something a little harder. You've earned it. Talk to you after the New Year, kid."

She stared into her phone. Stan had hung up and gone on to his celebration, or wherever he was actually headed.

New Year's.

That left her more than a week to be at loose ends. Her parents, from their last mass mailing that had gone not just to her sisters and her, but to colleagues and friends, as well, had said they were on their way to ——ched island for the holidays.

According to other missives, her sisters had each opted to be out of town, as well, after exhausting the social party circuit they always frequented this time of year.

What that boiled down to was that there was no one to come home to in San Francisco.

For a second, Kim thought about where that left her: idle and alone.

She supposed she could take Garrett and Jackson up on their hospitality. Today at breakfast, Garrett had told her to stay as long as she needed to and Jackson had seconded that sentiment. The latter had even pointed out that since his wife was a nurse, her ankle—which was already doing a lot better than she had anticipated it would—would be attended to on a regular basis.

All the bases were covered.

The longer you stay, the harder it's going to be to leave, a little voice in her head whispered. Damn it, she thought, Miss Joan had been right.

Think about this later, she ordered herself.

A lot of people would have given anything to be where she was—a cocoon surrounded by a warm, stitched-together family of people who cared, nestled in a town of good, decent people who would have gone out of their way for her. People she would have done anything for.

She sat there, perfectly still, almost afraid to breathe, as the realization that had just dawned on her slowly sank in.

She *cared* about these people—and they had been good to her when they clearly didn't have to be.

There had to be a way to pay them back for that. A way to show Jackson and Garrett how grateful she was that they had taken her in so effortlessly when they could have, just as easily, let her stay in her hotel room.

The best way to pay them back was to make sure that the ranch they both loved so much didn't wind up going under.

Since Jackson had vetoed her idea about franchising the Healing Ranch, she had to come up with another way the brothers could become, and remain, solvent.

"How ABOUT KIDS with disabilities?" she cried as she made her way into the den a little while later. She'd been looking for Garrett so she could tell him about her new idea and the search hadn't been easy for her. Making herself use one of the crutches despite the pain, she'd hobbled through half the house—or so it had felt— before she'd finally located him.

On his feet instantly, Garrett approached her so that he could carry her over to a chair. But he stopped midway when he saw the look in her eyes. Whatever else she was talking about, making her way into the room was a matter of pride. He allowed her to maintain it.

"What about them?" Garrett asked, then, before she said anything, he pointed out the obvious. "You've really got to stop starting your sentences in the middle of your thoughts. Some of us aren't as quick as you are and you need to spell things out for us." He ended his suggestion with a smile that was meant to warm her heart. "Now, what about kids with disabilities?"

"You could help them the same way you did me," she told him with enthusiasm.

All he could think of was the way she had been in his arms last night.

"I'm pretty sure there's a law against that," he told

her, mischief plainly gleaming in his eyes and abundantly evident in the expression on his face.

"No, I mean with the horses," she told him, shaking her head adamantly. "You know, showing them how to care for their horse, or just how to get the horse to obey certain commands that they give. That would go a long way to making those kids feel that they're more than just their disabilities. It gives them *hope*," she emphasized. "It shows them that they can conquer what they felt had conquered them and go on to *be* useful people." Kim sighed, frustrated. In her excitement, her words were all coming out jumbled. "I'm not saying this very well—I'm better on paper."

He came up to her and put his hands lightly on her shoulders, subtly holding her up just in case her weight caused her ankle to give way.

"You're saying it *very* well, and you're not better on paper," he admonished. "You're better on a bed sheet," Garrett informed her with a wink that caused her stomach muscles to tighten in response.

She frowned. "I'm serious."

"So am I." Then, for her sake, he attempted to look a little more solemn as he went on, "And for the record, I think this idea might actually appeal to Jackson. It would mean expanding the ranch to help accommodate this new area," he theorized. "We'd need more people working with the kids."

Kim's suggestion quickly began to take on depth and breadth in his mind. She just might have hit on a solution after all, he couldn't help thinking. "Jackson and I can handle the troubled teens who come here, but those other kids, that's going to take someone with a gift for reaching them."

The second he said that, the possible solution came to her. "It might only take the teens you work with."

Momentarily lost in thought, Garrett had only half heard her. "How's that again?"

"Well, maybe not all of them," she said, refining her answer. "But it stands to reason that you're training those boys to bury their aggressive feelings and focus on training their horses. Once they get the hang of that, why can't they go on and work with the kids with disabilities? Under qualified supervision, of course, but still, they could be your foot soldiers in all this. Nothing reinforces a lesson more than having to go over it again by passing it on."

He laughed and impulsively hugged her, pulling her to him, albeit gently. He was careful not to accidentally damage the progress her ankle had made.

"You're an absolute genius, Kim. That's terrific! The whole thing's a great idea!" he said with unbridled enthusiasm.

He couldn't have said anything that would have made her happier—except, perhaps, for a three-word sentence. She instantly dismissed that, calling herself greedy. She had to enjoy what she had, not want more.

"Let's just say I work well under pressure and when I'm inspired," she told him.

Damn, but he could have devoured her right here and now. Instead, he tried to appease himself by just holding her to him.

"Which is this?" he asked her.

"A little of both," she admitted, then added, "I really wanted to pay you and Jackson back a little for putting up with me."

"No need for that," he told her honestly. "Jackson feels good about going the extra mile."

Garrett hugged her again, thinking how good it felt to have her against him like this. Wishing with all his heart that there was a way that this could always be this way.

But she was independent and feisty, and he was afraid that if he tried to convince her to stay, she'd think he was attempting to clip her wings. If she thought that, he knew she'd take off that much sooner.

He was just going to have to content himself with taking—and enjoying—this one day at a time.

CRUSHED AGAINST HIS CHEST, Kim moved her head so that she could better listen to his heartbeat—the sound of it had an extremely calming effect.

When she finally opened her eyes again, for the first time she noticed something hanging from the ceiling. Moving her head back a little to get a better view, she pointed upward and asked, "What's that?"

Garrett didn't have to look up. He saw where her finger was pointing. He'd just hung it up in the den less than an hour ago, hoping for a moment just like this. Because she had burst into the den—or her version of bursting at any rate, he'd held off doing anything.

But she had just given him a perfect excuse.

"It's a mistletoe," he told her. "You can't tell me that a smart journalist like yourself doesn't know a mistletoe when she sees one."

Actually, she had never bothered learning what the holiday sprig looked like. She'd had no interest in frivolous outward signs of the holiday season like that. Until now.

"I know a smooth talker when I see one," she countered, avoiding a direct answer to his question.

"Then I'll expect you to point him or her out to me when you see them," he responded with the straightest face he could manage. "Me, I'm just a simple lover of nature and a firm believer in upholding traditions. By the way, the tradition around here is that if you find yourself standing beneath a mistletoe, you'll either kiss someone or be kissed by someone."

She looked at Garrett with the most innocent expression she could summon and asked, "There're only two choices?"

He thought for a moment, then allowed, "There's a third."

Her interest piqued as to what he'd come up with, she asked, "Which is?"

"The people beneath the mistletoe can both kiss each other."

Her warm smile spread until it encompassed all of her—as well as him. "I like that one best."

"I'm glad," he told her, adding, "because I like it, too."

She laced her arms around the back of his neck, drawing in closer. "How's that old expression go again? Put your money where your mouth is?" she asked him, pretending not to be sure that she had gotten the wording right.

"I know it well," he assured her.

"Good. Then prove it," she instructed.

Garrett's arms tightened around her as he did just that.

Epilogue

"No, really, it's all right," Kim said, attempting to beg off. "I'll be fine. I'll just have something in my room."

Garrett looked at her uncertainly. Was this her way of distancing herself from him? Was she leaving sooner than she'd told him the other day? He'd thought he had until New Year's Day to subtly get her to change her mind.

He was going to have to step up his game plan, he told himself.

"Why would you want to stay holed up in your room while everyone's out here? It's not like we haven't all seen you eat," he told her.

She looked at him, confused. "What does the way I eat have to do with anything?"

He shrugged. "I don't know, but it's the only reason I could come up with why you don't want to join us for Christmas Eve dinner."

It was a lie, but he wasn't about to bring up all the things that were plaguing him. He was out to eliminate them, not call attention to them.

The truth was she felt awkward around such an abundance of warmth and caring, covert or otherwise. It just reminded her of everything she hadn't had and wouldn't have once she left here. Despite the fact that she had grown up in the lap of luxury, she'd grown up poor, she realized now.

Poor in the things that counted.

She fell back on a generic excuse. "Because I'd feel like I'm intruding on your personal time. Christmas is for families."

Garrett began to see through her resistance—and he started to relax. This might just turn out well after all. "Haven't you heard? It takes all kinds to make a family these days. Being part of a family is more of a feeling than a matter of biology." He pretended to fix her with a serious look. "Now, will you come along peacefully, or am I going to have to get tough?"

She smiled despite herself. "I guess I'll come along peacefully."

Garrett nodded. "Good choice." With that, he crossed over to her and swept her up in his arms.

"I can walk now," she reminded him. "Not well," she conceded, "but I can manage."

"Indulge me," he told her, heading for the stairs. "I like holding you in my arms like this. Besides, you know how Rosa gets if we're late for dinner."

"Rosa, huh?" Her mouth curved. "I thought Jackson was supposed to be the one who had strict rules about latecomers at the table."

"Jackson, Rosa, it's all one and the same. They're the authority figures around here, each king or queen of their own little kingdom."

It was an unspoken given. Rosa ruled the kitchen; Jackson was in charge of everywhere else.

Kim cocked her head, looking at his profile. "And what are you?"

Garrett shrugged off the question. "I'm just a lowly warrior."

"I think, in order to keep the analogy the same, you'd have to be a knight," she pointed out.

He stopped as he came to the bottom of the stairs with her. "I'll be whatever you want me to," he said, his eyes holding hers for a long moment.

She knew she was imagining things, but for just a sliver of a moment, she felt as if he was making her a promise.

The next moment, she shook the feeling off, telling herself she was being ridiculous. If anything, it was just wishful thinking on her part.

"Found her in her room," Garrett declared to the others who were already gathered around the dining room table.

The table itself was extended to accommodate a few extra faces. Some of the boys who had made significant strides during their stay at the Healing Ranch had gone on to make friends with teens in town and had permission to invite them to dinner tonight.

It was all, Jackson had said, part of the program, to integrate these teens into the flow of society.

As Garrett helped her onto a chair, he could see that she had taken note that there were others here, as well as the ones who were staying in the bunkhouse.

"See, you're not the outsider you thought you'd be here at the table," he whispered into her ear just before he withdrew to take his own seat beside her.

Though she gave no outward indication of it, Kim held on to the warm feeling his whisper had generated along her skin for as long as she could.

"You sure you had enough?" Garrett asked her for the third time as they left the table and made their way, along with everyone else, to the living room.

"If I had another bite, I'd be waddling into the living room instead of hopping."

"You don't have to do either if you let me carry you," he pointed out.

"I've got to get back to walking around on my own. I can't expect you to carry me everywhere I go," she pointed out.

He floored her by asking, "Why not?" as he helped her take a seat on the sofa.

"I'm serious," she pointed out.

"Maybe just a little too serious," he commented. When she looked at him quizzically, he reminded her, "This *is* Christmas Eve. It's okay to lighten up."

That wasn't the way Christmas Eve had been at her house when she'd been growing up, Kim recalled. Half the time, they weren't together. When they did happen to be under one roof for the occasion, it was predominantly a time of tension for her. A time of fearful anticipation that something would go wrong that night, and she would either do or say something to displease her parents and earn their dark looks and their barely veiled scorn.

"If you say so," she murmured, forcing a smile to her lips as she tried to banish old memories that threatened to swallow her up.

"I do," he answered. "My house, my rules." Then he glanced at his brother who was looking his way. Jackson was obviously thinking that the tables were turned and now it was *his* turn to squirm, Garrett thought, recalling how he had been on his brother's case until Jackson had gone to Debi to tell her how he felt and to ask her not to leave. "Our house," he amended. "Our rules."

"Okay." Kim obliged. In general, Garrett's house was a great deal nicer and warmer than her parents' mansion was.

The living room was also where Jackson and Garrett had put up the tree that everyone else on the ranch had helped decorate. There was a blanket of gifts beneath the tree now and as Jackson started reading off the names on the gifts, it became obvious to Kim that part of the tradition here at the ranch was to open gifts on Christmas Eve instead of on Christmas Day.

"Nice way to get a head start on the big day," she commented when Garrett sat down beside her.

Debi and Jackson had taken over distribution of the gifts. Garrett was content to sit right beside her and just look on, as long as she was right there with him.

The gifts were almost all distributed when Debi came over and placed a small square box on the long rectangular table right in front of Kim. "And this one's got your name on it," she said before getting back to the tree.

"My name?" Kim repeated, staring at the gift. "There has to be some mistake."

"No mistake. Unless your name's not Kim," she added.

"It is," she murmured. The next moment, she looked at Garrett. "I feel awful. I didn't get anyone anything."

"Not exactly true," Garrett contradicted. "That article you wrote gave the ranch a shot in the arm—and your idea for expanding it did even more. I told Jackson about it and he's thinking of getting that underway after the first of the year."

"Can't put a bow around that," she pointed out.

"Can't always put a bow around the best gifts," he told her.

She looked down at the box, thinking it couldn't possibly contain what it looked like it contained to her. Most likely, the box held a symbolic key to the ranch, to indicate that she was always welcomed here.

Those were the kind of people Garrett and his brother and Debi were, she thought, feeling just a little misty even before she got the wrapping paper off the box.

She was not prepared for what she found inside.

She felt the corners of her eyes growing damp before she could even form a single word. Unable to speak, she raised her eyes to Garrett's.

He took the tears to mean that she was disappointed. "I know it isn't exactly the traditional kind of ring, but it was my mother's. It was the only thing of worth my father ever gave her."

"That's not true," she told him hoarsely. "He gave her you."

His breath felt as if it had gotten stuck in his lungs, going neither in nor out. It took him a second to center himself. "Does that mean you're saying yes? Or is that your polite way of—"

"Yes, I'm saying yes," she cried, cutting him off. "If you're asking me to marry you, I'm saying yes. If you're not asking me to marry you, then I'm proposing, but either way, the answer *yes* is in there!" she cried.

Stunned, Garrett could only sit there, staring at her, utterly speechless until Jackson strode over to him and slapped the back of his head.

"Do it right and ask her. Don't just leave her hanging there," Jackson ordered. "She's already given you her answer."

"Kimberly Lee, I don't have much to offer you—"

"Wrong again," she interjected, laughing and crying at the same time as she threw her arms around his neck. "And the answer's still yes—so don't try to talk me out of it."

Garrett didn't remember glancing at his brother for guidance just then, but Jackson did give him his counsel. "Don't mess it up," he advised his younger brother. "Quit while you're ahead."

Garrett was already doing just that.

He'd stopped talking altogether. It was hard to talk and kiss at the same time, and he far preferred the latter to the former.

* * * * *